JACKIE CARREIRA is a writer, musician, designer, co-founder of QuirkHouse Theatre Company, and award-winning playwright. Born in Leicester, she moved to London as a baby and went to school in Hackney, but also spent part of her early childhood in Lisbon's Old Quarter. Destiny thereby dictated that her formative years were heavily influenced by her working-class upbringing and cities beginning with the letter 'L', for some cosmic reason that she has not yet figured out.

Jackie now lives in the English county of Suffolk with her actor husband AJ Deane, two cats and too many books. One of her favourite places to write is in railway cafés. *The Seventh Train* was originally born over several cappuccinos at Paddington station.

Suffolk contains no cities at all – not even one that begins with the letter 'L'. Your move, Destiny.

The
Seventh Train

Best wishes,

Jackie C.

Jackie Carreira

Matador
9 Priory Business Park,
Wistow Road, Kibworth Beauchamp,
Leicestershire. LE8 0RX
Tel: 0116 279 2299
Email: books@troubador.co.uk
Web: www.troubador.co.uk/matador
Twitter: @matadorbooks

ISBN 978 1789018 936

British Library Cataloguing in Publication Data.
A catalogue record for this book is available from the British Library.

Printed and bound in Great Britain by 4edge Limited
Typeset in 11pt Minion Pro by Troubador Publishing Ltd, Leicester, UK

Matador is an imprint of Troubador Publishing Ltd

"It's a great huge game of chess that's being played – all over the world – if this is the world at all, you know. Oh, what fun it is! How I wish I was one of them! I wouldn't mind being a Pawn, if only I might join."

(From *Through the Looking Glass* by Lewis Carroll)

Introduction

Writing *The Seventh Train* has been a journey in itself. The story began several years ago as a short, fifteen-minute play for theatre with two characters – the first play to be accepted for production at the start of my own journey as a playwright. It had its debut at the Fisher Theatre in Bungay, produced by the *Eyes Write* company in Norfolk, and it was a huge thrill to see characters come to life on stage that had once existed only in my mind. A year later, the same company performed it on local Norfolk radio, and another company for Suffolk radio. But the story hadn't finished with the writer.

From East Anglia, *The Seventh Train* took on another passenger and travelled to Berkshire. A third character had arrived, and the story had progressed to a half-hour, one act play. It was selected to be performed at the Windsor Fringe Festival, and was one of the winners of the *Kenneth Branagh 10th Anniversary Drama Award*. But the story still hadn't finished with the writer.

A fourth character got on board and *The Seventh Train* journeyed on to become a full-length stage play. It travelled back to East Anglia and had its debut in a small room above a bar in Bury St Edmunds, then departed for a tour around the county with *QuirkHouse Theatre Company*. But still, the story hadn't finished with the writer.

Finally, the characters moved from the stage to the page, picking up new passengers along the way. Today, *The Seventh Train* has arrived in your town, in your hands, so that you may be part of the journey for a while, if it is your pleasure to jump aboard. Has the story finally finished with the writer?... We'll see.

Bon Voyage!

Suffolk, 2019

DISCLAIMER: The train timetables in this novel are a work of fiction. Any resemblance to actual train timetables that might be considered by passengers to be works of fiction is entirely coincidental.

Chapter One:
The First Train from Harlow Town Station

This is a passenger announcement: Greater Anglia trains would like to apologise for the delay in the arrival of the ten-o-five service from London, Liverpool Street. This is due to a passenger on the line at Harlow Town. We would like to apologise for any inconvenience.

The announcement that crackled over the tannoy at Cambridge station was not a recording. Those kinds of announcements never are, despite their increasing regularity. It was read out by a man, perhaps in his fifties or sixties. However old he was, he sounded neither young nor inexperienced. His voice carried no extraneous emotion because it wasn't the first time he'd said the words 'passenger on the line' into the station office microphone. It was, in fact, the fifth time this year – and it was only February. Elizabeth could have been on her way to Cambridge by now, but she wasn't. She was stuck at Harlow Town.

The announcement could mean that some fool had been messing around on the train lines with no thought or care for the inconvenience of others. It could mean that some hero had jumped down onto the tracks, to rescue a puppy or perhaps an injured pigeon, with no thought or care for their own safety. It could mean that some clumsy commuter had slipped between the train and the platform – not minding the gap at all – when impatient travellers pushed forward to claim a precious seat. Or it could mean that somebody had deliberately thrown themselves in front of a moving train, hoping to end their troubled life quickly and with minimal pain. This morning, it was the last scenario.

At this rate, Elizabeth wouldn't be at Cambridge for ages yet. She'd travelled through a lot of railway stations, so the risk of coming across this kind of thing was pretty high. She was at the opposite end of the platform when it happened, which meant that she didn't see it, but she did hear it. Everybody at the station did. Fortunately for her, and all the other passengers waiting on the platform, what Elizabeth heard was the wailing screech of emergency brakes rather than the gruesome thud of metal hitting flesh and bone. What she smelled was the burning of brakes and the discharge of diesel fumes rather than blood. What she saw was mercifully very little.

A crowd had gathered at the far end of the platform as high-vis station staff tried in vain to push them back. Within moments Elizabeth could see mobile phones raised in the air all around, frantically pointing and clicking at anything that could be shared later on Facebook pages or tweeted out into the virtual world. It made Elizabeth feel sick. The phones continued to buzz and flash around the unfolding tragedy like hungry flies as she turned and walked to the station café.

A bare-armed, busty woman was behind the counter, wiping down the surfaces with a pine-stinking cloth. She was the only other person in the café. Anyone else who had been in there was now outside with the rest of the flies. "Morning," said the woman.

"'Good morning," said Elizabeth. "Could I have a black coffee, please?"

"Regular or large?"

"Regular is fine, thanks."

The woman put down the cloth and set about preparing the coffee. She scanned Elizabeth up and down as she worked, analysing her over her shoulder as she liked to do with all her customers: 'He's a wrong 'un; She's all fur coat and no knickers; He's a con man's dream…' that kind of thing; trapping strangers in clichés like butterflies under glass. Elizabeth didn't realise she was being scrutinised. She was conveniently avoiding eye contact by fishing in her bag for her purse. "It's all going on out there." The woman threw the remark away like a used tissue.

"Yes, I suppose it is." Elizabeth didn't really want to talk but convention dictated she should interact, at least until her coffee was ready.

"You're lucky, love. We had a queue six deep in here just now. You'd have been waiting ten minutes for me to serve you, if all *that* wasn't going on."

"I guess you could call it lucky," said Elizabeth. "I'm not sure I would."

The woman finished pouring the coffee and looked at her customer more squarely. There was something about her that she hadn't quite managed to pin down. Not yet. She tested her a little. "You're not one of those rubber-neckers, then?"

"Sorry?"

3

"Like that mob out there." She stabbed her fat thumb in the direction of the platform. "Taking pictures now, are they?"

"Yes, they are. And no, I'm definitely not one of them." Elizabeth looked directly into the woman's eyes for the first time. They were pale blue and too piercing for Elizabeth to be able to penetrate behind them comfortably with her own, dark brown eyes. Her gaze turned downwards again as she pretended to count the coins in her purse.

The woman continued regardless. "It's disgusting. I've seen too many of them, poor sods. Your last desperate act on God's Earth and you're surrounded by tossers taking selfies." She punctuated the last word by putting the coffee down a little too hard on the counter, spilling some hot, dark liquid onto the freshly-wiped surface. "Revolting, don't you think?"

"I do indeed," agreed Elizabeth. "What do I owe you?"

"Two-pound-fifty, love."

Elizabeth counted out the correct change and handed it over. The woman's palm was warm and still moist from the cleaning cloth. Elizabeth offered a smile just wide enough to be polite. "Thank you," she said, then moved to a table as far away from the counter as possible and sat down.

'That's it! She's running away from something,' thought the woman. 'Probably some bad relationship. Typical men. They're all the bloody same.' Then, satisfied that her latest customer had been properly stuffed into a pigeon-hole, she sprayed some more pine-stinking liquid onto the counter and scrubbed with renewed vigour.

It was a good few minutes before a gaggle of passengers entered the café, bringing with them a clatter of noise and disruption. Strangers talked to strangers a little too loudly and with too much familiarity, as they always do in these situations: "What a way to go." "I only saw his shoe." "I'm going to be late for work – again." "Must have been desperate, poor thing." "Why can't they just kill themselves in private? Selfish bastards." And so on and so on and so on. Elizabeth fetched a well-thumbed paperback from her canvas shopping bag and hid her face behind it. Nobody noticed her. A voice from the tannoy cut across the chatter.

> *Greater Anglia trains would like to apologise for the cancellation of the ten-thirty-eight service to Cambridge. This is due to a fatality on the line, which is currently being dealt with by emergency services. The next train to depart from platform one will now be delayed by approximately forty-five minutes. We would like to apologise to customers for any inconvenience.*

'Inconvenience.' The word echoed around Elizabeth's brain. Someone chose to hurl themselves in front of a moving train this morning. Someone just ended their life like a bug on a windscreen and their first obituary was that they were an 'inconvenience' to others. It was beyond tragic.

There was a time, not too long ago, when Elizabeth might have become an inconvenience herself. She chose to reason that she hadn't been brave enough to jump because it was less troubling for her to think of it that way. Now, sitting in the café at Harlow Town station, she mused upon the notion that she might be a coward but at least she'd never been an inconvenience to others.

She'd have to flick back a few pages in her novel. Her eyes had only been skimming the printed words and she hadn't taken anything in at all. It wasn't a bad story – a family saga of mothers and sons in war-torn countries. She'd found the book yesterday, discarded on a train seat in the quiet carriage. Perhaps a passenger forgot it in their hurry to get somewhere, or perhaps they'd finished it and were passing it on. Some people do that. However it got there, Elizabeth was grateful. She always loved to find books on trains. In rare moments of playfulness, she liked to imagine it was the god of literature leaving her a gift. She would then, in turn, leave a toffee as an offering. It was one of her little luxuries to always carry a small pack of toffees in her handbag.

The next train was going to be delayed for a while. The announcement said 'forty-five minutes' but, in Elizabeth's experience, train companies tended to over-promise and under-deliver. It was still quite early. Perhaps she should get out of the station and take a stroll around Harlow Town. She'd never been there before. Maybe there was somewhere interesting where she could lose a couple of hours – a museum or a gallery would be nice. Or maybe there was a nice little bed and breakfast nearby. She could check in and resume her journey in the morning. Nobody was waiting for her. There was nowhere to be at any particular time. 'Yes, that's what I'll do,' she thought. 'I'll find somewhere clean to stay, get a good rest, have a shower, and come back in the morning. Maybe I'll still end up in Cambridge.' Elizabeth slid her book back into her shopping bag, drained the last of her coffee, and walked out of the café, leaving the human flies still buzzing behind her.

At the far end of the station platform, transport police and paramedics were doing their jobs like they always do. It was too late to save the young man, who had died almost instantly, just as he had hoped. In the inside pocket of his black leather jacket was a polite note addressed to 'The driver of the train.' It read: 'Dear Sir or Madam, I'm sorry.' And that was all it said.

The driver of the ten-o-five from London, Liverpool Street was sitting in the station office wrapped in a blanket, shaking and staring in shock. His name was Daniel Cotter and he was a third-generation train driver. His grandfather was one of the *Windrush* men who'd come to England from Jamaica looking for a job for life. He found one on the railways and died of a heart attack three weeks after he retired. It had indeed been a job for life; a life that was ultimately too short and too hard. His gold-plated watch, inscribed on the back with his name and the train company's logo, he left to his son, Peter. By then, Peter was following in his father's footsteps and was the proudest man alive when, a few years later, his own son, Daniel, had decided to do the same. Neither of the first two Cotter men had ever killed another human being; neither with a train nor with anything else.

A female police officer was sitting next to Daniel, her well-trained hand resting on his shoulder, waiting patiently to take a full statement before they could complete all the paperwork that emanates from incidents like these. He hadn't seen the letter to 'The driver of the train.' The police officer had it in her pocket. Letters like that are taken away for evidence.

That had been the third life that his train had cut short – one for each generation of the Cotter family. It was time for Daniel to re-think his own life.

Chapter Two:
Cambridge Station

This is a passenger safety announcement. Please ensure that all luggage and personal items are kept with you at all times and report any suspicious activity to staff at the station security office. Thank you for travelling with us today.

It was the same recorded voice on all the safety announcements at all of the stations on the Greater Anglia rail network. Perhaps she was an out-of-work actress, trained at some London drama school to have the right kind of plummy voice; the right balance of politeness and total authority. Or maybe she was some lucky railway employee, singled out for tannoy fame for her deadpan clarity and non-offensive accent. She did it rather well.

Cambridge station is relatively small, considering the number of students, commuters and tourists who file through it every day. Despite its size, and like all railway stations in towns and cities across the Western world, there were multiple opportunities to buy coffee.

Elizabeth had made it to Cambridge after a good night's sleep in a relatively cheap, surprisingly clean hotel in Harlow. Now she was waiting for her next train in the café on the main platform, rather than grabbing a takeaway from one of the kiosks and trying to find a spare seat on a cold bench. It was a bit quieter in the café. It's a reliable rule of thumb that those in a hurry make more noise, so the sit-down coffee shops in stations tend to attract those who have time to stop and wait; perhaps to read a little or check on how the world is doing through the screen of a smart phone. Elizabeth didn't own a mobile phone, smart or otherwise. Not anymore. The last time the battery ran out of charge, she'd simply left it, silent and dead, at some other railway station. She thought that somebody must have picked it up by now. She didn't bother to wonder who it might be. Maybe it was sitting abandoned in some lost property office with all the umbrellas and books and empty wallets. If it was, they were welcome to it.

The café in Cambridge station was busy and Elizabeth had only just managed to grab the last free table. She didn't carry much baggage, just a handbag and her sturdy, canvas shopping bag containing a few items of clothing and other replaceable essentials. She placed the shopping bag on one of the two spare chairs at her table. It was meant to dissuade others from sitting there, allowing strangers to assume the space was being saved for someone, at least until one of those terrifying moments when another traveller might challenge for the right to sit. The strap of her handbag was firmly stretched from one shoulder to the opposite hip because it contained her most important things: money and bank cards, a toothbrush, a hairbrush, her railway season ticket, and whatever paperback she'd most recently been gifted by the god of literature. She thought about reserving the other spare chair with her handbag, but decided it was much too precious to be that far away from her. Instead, she would take off her coat and drape it casually over the back of the seat, pretending it belonged to someone else; someone who might be at the counter or in the toilets. Before she could pull her first arm free of its stiff, woollen sleeve, a man's voice, close behind her, stopped her in her tracks. It was the question she most hated, and the one she was deliberately trying to avoid.

"Excuse me, is this chair free?"

Elizabeth turned her head awkwardly, her right arm hanging half out of her coat. She saw the face of a man, about her age and bronzed as if he'd just been on holiday. He wore an expensive-looking hat, modelled on a traditional trilby in black with cream flecks. A white, embroidered logo featured on the side – no more than a squiggle – that marked the hat out as so exclusive that only those who could afford it could recognise it. Elizabeth certainly didn't. The rest of his clothes looked casually expensive but creased. This man was a stranger to an ironing board. His voice sounded younger than his face looked, and he was self-assured and smiling, like he practiced looking confident in a mirror before leaving the house. Elizabeth was caught off guard. "Oh, errm... do you mean *this* chair?"

The man smiled a little more roundly, as if he'd found the question quaint and amusing. "Yes – if you don't mind, that is."

"Oh, I'd rather you didn't." Elizabeth slid her arm back into her coat sleeve and tried to regain her composure. "I prefer to sit alone, if you don't mind." Then she added an unnecessary 'sorry' for good measure.

The man tilted his head a little to one side. Elizabeth couldn't tell if it was done from resentment or pity. His persistent smile gave nothing away. "I meant can I take this chair? If no-one else is sitting here, that is."

Elizabeth noticed then that the man had been pointing towards another table nearby that had just become vacant. There was one chair there already. Perhaps, unlike her, he actually *was* waiting for someone else. She felt her cheeks getting hot. Misfired assumptions have the ability to heat the blood very efficiently. "Oh, of course. I'm so sorry. I thought you wanted to sit."

"I do," said the man, "but over there." His smile became wider and spread to his eyes. Elizabeth's cheeks just got hotter.

With increasing embarrassment, she could only repeat her apology. "I'm so sorry. Nothing personal," she said. "Take the chair, please."

The man bent and picked up the chair in one hand with surprising deftness. The other hand had been gripping a large, foaming cup of coffee the whole time. "Thank you very much," he said. And then, as a seemingly throwaway afterthought, he added: "Don't forget to keep your eyes open for suspicious activity."

Elizabeth frowned and rested her hand firmly on her handbag, holding it even closer to her chest. "I beg your pardon?"

"Just a joke. You know, the station announcement," and then he proffered an appalling impression of the disembodied woman with the perfect voice: "Please report any suspicious activity to station staff…" Then he winked and let out a snort of a laugh that was far too big for his small joke. "Can't be too careful these days, can we?"

Elizabeth agreed. The man with the hat paused for a moment. He looked as if he was waiting for her to ask a question, or maybe share a laugh with him. She stubbornly did neither. "Right," he said, "I'll just take the chair then," and carefully balancing his coffee in one hand and the chair in the other, the man made his way back towards the empty table. Elizabeth tried very hard not to watch him, but she couldn't help herself. Putting the coffee down first, the man carefully placed the second chair precisely opposite the one that was already waiting at the table. Then he sat on the first, put his feet up on the second with a sigh of contentment, pulled a small black notebook and pen from his jacket pocket and began to write. Before Elizabeth could force herself to turn away, the man looked up and straight into her eyes. He threw her a quick wink then put his head down to scribble some more.

The next train to depart from platform five is the twelve-twenty-one service to King's Lynn, calling at Ely, Downham Market, Watlington and King's Lynn. Platform five for the next train to King's Lynn.

"Two," said Elizabeth. She said it out loud under her breath, staring up at the disembodied announcement as if the woman with the perfect voice was hanging on the wall. She said the word quietly so that no-one else could hear, but her lips moved unconsciously as she spoke. The man with the hat didn't hear what she said, but he *saw* her say something that looked odd. He couldn't be sure. It might have been anything, but it did look like she said 'two.'

Elizabeth fetched the novel from her bag, opened it at the page with the most recently folded-down corner, and started to read. It wasn't her train that was about to depart from platform five. She had a little while to wait yet. The man with the hat studied her face. She was about the same age as him but appeared to be trying desperately to hide it. Not the way that most women in their forties do by making up and dressing like they did at the peak of their physical attractiveness – usually around twenty-five years old. The eyelids and hands always give it away, no matter how polished the nails or how thick the mascara. Later it's the neck and the knees. This woman was doing the opposite. It was as if she was trying to be invisible at best, and downright dowdy at worst. Her clothes bore no logos or frippery, just muted colours in rectangular shapes that only hinted at the curves of a female form underneath. She wore no make-up but her skin was blemish-free. A few faint lines radiated from the outer corners of her eyes, and a few more slid down from the sides of her nose to the edges of her mouth, but they were the only remarkable features. Right now, there was no expression on her face and the lack of wrinkles suggested that this was the normal state of affairs. Her hair was dark and curly, pulled back into a tight ponytail. A few wisps hung down and tickled her forehead. Every now and then she brushed them back off her face with almost mechanical movements.

The man with the hat studied Elizabeth just a tiny bit longer. He didn't want his gaze to linger on her for too long in case she started to feel it on her skin and stare back. He believed that was possible; that vision was sticky and that looks could glue themselves to people. It happened all

14

the time. He crinkled his brow into a pensive frown then put his head down and scribbled into his notebook some more. He didn't see the girl come in at first, but he heard her. The whole café did.

"Excuse me, babe. Do you mind if I sit here?"

For the second time in five minutes, Elizabeth's worst café nightmare had come to life. She looked up from her paperback to see a young woman with an over-cheerful face, a large cappuccino in one hand and a huge suitcase on wheels in the other. The suitcase was emblazoned with multi-coloured hearts and looked overstuffed to bursting point. "Not again," said Elizabeth, but she said it louder than she meant to.

The girl heard her. "Sorry?" she said.

Elizabeth rushed to cover her unintentional rudeness by being far more polite than she needed to be. "No, *I'm* sorry. I didn't mean to be rude, it's just that, if you don't mind, I'd prefer to sit on my own, if that's OK… I'm *really* sorry."

The girl's cheeriness dropped a notch, along with the volume of her voice, but she persisted. "I'll be quiet as a mouse, and I promise I'm not mental or anything."

"It's not that, it's just…" Elizabeth paused to try and figure out what it 'just' was. It gave the girl a chance to press further.

"There's no empty tables in here and I need to put this flippin' coffee down. It's really, really hot!" She placed the cappuccino down on the table and flicked the heat from her fingers over-dramatically. "Unless you're saving the seat for someone else?"

Elizabeth couldn't think of any reasonable arguments quickly enough. The girl looked at her with wide, kitten-eyes that dared to be denied. Elizabeth moved her shopping bag off its chair and tucked it under the table between her feet. "No, that's fine," she conceded, pulling out the empty chair. "Please, help yourself."

"Phew! Thank you *so* much." With some difficulty, the girl manoeuvred the heavy suitcase between the precious chair and Elizabeth, then sat herself down heavily. "I tell you what, it is soooo flippin' good to sit down." She slid her coffee towards the centre of the table and lifted her large, pink shoulder bag onto her lap. She exhaled a satisfied sigh, opened the bag and proceeded to pull out a mobile phone in a sequinned case, some lip gloss, a pair of red sunglasses, a folding mirror, and a paper bag hiding some newly-purchased item. The colourful assortment clattered noisily across the table's metal surface. The whole time, Elizabeth had kept her nose buried in her book and was pretending, with increasing futility, that she was still alone. It was impossible. The girl shifted the suitcase towards herself and dumped her now half-empty shoulder bag on top of it. "This case weighs a flippin' ton," she said, as if Elizabeth had asked. "I always pack too much. I suppose it's a girlie thing, isn't it? Don't want to be caught with the wrong shoes on, do I?"

"I guess not," said Elizabeth, trying hard not to look up, which wasn't easy. This entertaining little display was magnetic to the eyes.

It was obvious that the girl had no intention of being as quiet as a mouse, and she continued babbling without a trace of remorse: "These are my favourite shoes." She lifted her feet off the floor and clicked her heels like a council house Dorothy. The shoes were red and shiny with white satin ribbons for laces and chunky, black Cuban heels. Elizabeth couldn't help but stare down at the footwear. They were the kind of over-priced items that impractically-dressed models wore in expensive magazines, or that shops paraded in the middle of window displays to make the other shoes look more interesting by proximity.

The girl took a sip of her coffee and grimaced. "Oh, for flip's sake! I forgot the sugar." She slapped herself on the wrist in mock reprimand. "I always forget something. I'm surprised I remembered the flippin' coffee, to be honest. Would you mind watching my stuff for a minute?"

Elizabeth put down her book. She had tried as politely as possible to make it clear that she was not open to socialising with strangers, but it wasn't working. She wasn't in the mood to converse, let alone babysit a suitcase. "Look, I don't know if I should because…"

"It's okay." The girl waved away Elizabeth's concerns. "I'm not a terrorist or anything. I'd have worn more boring shoes if I was – Ha ha! That's how you can tell, you know. They never think about the shoes. Won't be a sec." The girl stood up, looking around the busy café.

Neither of them noticed the man with the hat walking over. He was carrying a little white bowl filled with sachets of sugar and artificial sweeteners that had been sitting on his table. He held out the bowl to the girl. "Need some of this?"

He had caught both women by surprise. "Oh, cool," said the girl, taking the bowl of sugar gratefully. "Thank you very much, kind sir," and she offered him a little curtsey before sitting back down.

17

"Don't mention it." The man touched his expensive hat in salute, turned with a flourish, went back to his table, and took up scribbling in his notebook once more. Elizabeth felt a pang of mild alarm. Maybe he was just being polite. Maybe she was being over-sensitive. Either way, she didn't like this sudden invasion that seemed to be coming at her from all her sides.

The girl leaned in towards Elizabeth in a confidential manner, concealing a pending comment behind the palm of one hand. She looked like a caricature; some comic book cutie. Harmless but comedic. "Bit observant, isn't he?" she whispered.

"Yes, he is," agreed Elizabeth. "A bit *too* observant for my liking."

The girl took three sachets of brown sugar from the bowl. "Still, good of him to bring it over, I suppose." She emptied the sachets into her cappuccino and checked around the table for a spoon. She couldn't find one so she stirred the hot coffee gingerly with her finger, licked it clean, and took a sip of the foamy liquid. "That's better." She took a deep breath in, raised her arms suddenly above her head, then let them drop back slowly to her sides. "And breathe... and calm." She repeated the exercise twice more while everyone in the café pretended not to notice.

Elizabeth gazed back down at her book. She had stopped reading several pages ago. She'd have to flick back a few when the girl wasn't looking. At the moment, she *was* looking. It was nothing more than friendly curiosity, but it made Elizabeth feel trapped. She glanced up at the digital departure board on the wall of the café. It wasn't time to go out on the platform yet. There were still a few trains to go. The idea of de-camping to the station waiting room crossed her mind, but it was probably just as full of people in there. At least in here she had a seat.

"I hope I'm not disturbing you or nothing." The girl was unable or unwilling to see the irony of her statement.

Elizabeth held her book firm and resisted raising her eyes from it. "Whatever gave you that idea?" She didn't mean to be sarcastic, but that's how it came out. The girl was as hopeless at recognising sarcasm as she was at spotting irony. Elizabeth's comment floated harmlessly over her head, missing her brain by several inches.

"I just needed to put this stuff down," she continued. "I could have sat over there, I guess, but the sugar bloke looked a bit… weird, you know?"

"There's a lot of it about." Elizabeth genuinely meant it.

"You're not kidding." The girl folded her arms and tutted loudly. "And I don't think he should have his flippin' feet on the chair neither, should he?"

"Maybe he's saving it for someone."

"Or maybe he's got no flippin' manners. Some people were thrown up, not brought up, don't you think?"

"I do indeed." Elizabeth was still looking resolutely down at her book. She flicked over a page to make it look like she was still reading. That's one more page to turn back and read again. 'If this carries on for much longer,' she thought, 'I'll have to go right back to the beginning.' She determined to do just that once she got on her train. The thought relaxed her a little and she gave herself up to just resting her eyes on the print.

The girl had been gazing aimlessly around the café with occasional sideways glances at Elizabeth, looking for an opportunity to speak or some kind of sign of openness to conversation. She took a sip of coffee, picked a speck of something from under a shiny blue fingernail with another shiny blue fingernail, then gazed around the café some more. She didn't have a novel to read, or even to pretend to read, and she was getting bored. The girl took a chance and pushed her face in towards Elizabeth again. "I love railway stations, don't you?"

Elizabeth leaned back a little, away from the threat of further personal space invasion. She decided to throw a response casually across the table in the hope that it would satisfy the girl and not lead to further discussion. "There are certainly worse places to be."

"You're telling me." The girl took the response, albeit a reluctant one, as an invitation to unleash some of the excitement and chatter that she'd been holding inside. It all came out in an animated gush. "I think it's the beginning and end of all those journeys, d'you know what I mean? I mean, it's like all these people are going somewhere or coming home or meeting someone. It's all a big adventure. I reckon they've all got a story to tell, don't you? Well, I do. It's all so flippin' fascinating, isn't it?" The girl finally took a breath.

Elizabeth could only echo half-heartedly. "Fascinating."

"God, yeah!… My name's Ellie, by the way."

The girl held out an open hand so that it hovered over Elizabeth's book. It would be too cruel to ignore it, and cruelty wasn't in Elizabeth's nature. She looked at the girl properly for the first time. Her face was round and open; a little over-made-up, like too many young women who really don't need it. Her hair was too straight to be entirely natural, but her smile was genuine and warm and begging to be returned. Elizabeth could do nothing but comply. She put down her book, not even bothering to mark the page she hadn't read, and shook the girl's waiting hand. "Nice to meet you, Ellie," she said.

The girl's smile seemed to spread throughout her whole being and spill out over the table as she eagerly shook Elizabeth's hand. She had the kind of radiance when she smiled that can only come from innocence. Or maybe it was naivety. Elizabeth judged it to be the latter. She could forgive that in a young woman like this. Ellie released Elizabeth's hand and relaxed back into her chair. "I've got two whole weeks to kill. Fourteen days. Sixteen, if you count both weekends."

"Very nice."

"Yep. I'm gonna start off in Brighton, then who knows? The world is my lobster! I go: Cambridge – King's Cross – St Pancras – Brighton – who knows? I'm up for an adventure. What about you, babes?"

If she was being forced to converse with another human being today, Elizabeth thought it might as well be a harmless one like Ellie. "I don't know yet," she replied with all honesty.

Ellie frowned. "How do you mean, you don't know?"

Before Elizabeth had a chance to give a plausible answer, Ellie's mobile phone sprang to life, rattling the metal table with its harsh vibrations. It rang with one of those non-descript dance tunes that only people under twenty-five can distinguish from all the other non-descript dance tunes. "Oops! Here we go." Ellie picked up the phone, checked the incoming number and swiped her finger across the screen. "Hi mum... No, not yet... I've only just flippin' left, haven't I?... Yes, I will... No, I promise. Don't forget to feed Percy... Yes, I promise. Call you when I get there... I know, I will... Okay, bye... bye... bye!" She hung up and put the phone back on the table with all the other random paraphernalia. Elizabeth tried hard not to watch her during the call, but the girl was so pleasantly animated, with accompanying little glances and eye rolls at Elizabeth, that she couldn't help but enjoy the diversion. "Sorry about that," said Ellie. "It's a bit rude, isn't it? And there I was having a go at sugar bloke for having no manners."

"It's okay," shrugged Elizabeth. "Don't worry about it."

"And I wasn't even thrown up! Believe it or not, my mum taught me manners." She continued, imitating her mother's voice with mock maturity: "'Ellie,' she says, 'life is very expensive but manners cost you nothing.'" And then, for additional clarity: "She's Irish, but I can't do the accent."

"I'll have to use my imagination," said Elizabeth, allowing herself a quiet chuckle of amusement.

Ellie hardly paused for breath. "But she worries about me, bless her. I'm not used to travelling on my own. I'm not gonna lie, it's a little bit scary, but I wouldn't tell her that. She'd only flippin' worry even more than she does already." Ellie stroked the paper bag on the table wistfully. "I just booked two weeks off work, packed my little bag – we'll quite a big bag actually – and here I am. I don't even know where I'm sleeping tonight. Flippin' crazy, ain't it?!" She paused to take another sip of cappuccino.

"Crazy," echoed Elizabeth flatly. She was still deciding whether to indulge this over-effusive young woman or make some excuse and leave. She could go and buy something at the newsagents or hide in the toilets. No, that would be a last resort. She decided to be patient and sit it out. In any case, Ellie's train would be here soon enough. The truth was that she was intrigued by the girl but didn't want to admit it to herself. Was Elizabeth ever that enthusiastic at her age? She couldn't remember if she was. It seemed like another lifetime ago.

Ellie put down her coffee and patted the overstuffed suitcase for emphasis. "I've got my toothbrush, spare underwear – what more does a girl need?" Elizabeth looked at the suitcase and raised her eyebrows. "OK," Ellie admitted. "Maybe some mascara and a bit of lippy, a couple of pairs of shoes." She counted the rest off on her fingers. "… skinny jeans, onesie, hair straighteners, maybe a couple of other bits and pieces for emergencies. Who knows? I might meet the man of my dreams. You've got to be ready." Ellie shrugged then hooted loudly at her own childlike optimism. She took another sip of coffee then remembered her manners. "Sorry babes, where did you say you were going?"

Elizabeth decided to reply to the straight question with a straight answer. "I don't know yet."

"Oh. Are you meeting someone off a train?" Ellie's expression changed at the fleeting thought that she might be intruding after all. "Oops! Were you really saving this chair?"

"No, I'm not meeting anyone." Elizabeth sipped some of her own coffee. It had gone cold. She thought about getting another but that had been her third today, and it was still early. She slid the coffee cup away from herself, inadvertently pushing Ellie's phone back towards the girl's side of the metal table. Ellie took it as a statement of rejection and looked mortified. She picked up the phone and slid it into her shoulder bag. Elizabeth hadn't meant any offence. She smiled at Ellie, an 'it's okay, really' kind of smile, and pulled the coffee cup back. She drained the last bit of cold, bitter liquid then pushed the cup out to the edge of the table where it could do no more harm.

"I didn't mean to be nosey, honest. Just passing the time, you know. My dad told me not to talk to strangers, but then he says I never flippin' listen to a word he says anyway." Ellie gathered her things together one by one and piled them neatly on top of the paper bag, all except the cappuccino that she now wrapped her fingers around for some kind of warm comfort. "These tables are very small, aren't they?"

Elizabeth put her cup very deliberately back in the middle of the table, making sure that Ellie saw. "Yes, they are."

Ellie beamed and moved her own cup next to Elizabeth's. All was now equal. Any misunderstanding was now understood and Ellie felt clear to proceed. "It's supposed to be a cool place, Brighton. I've never been there before. Have you?"

"Not for a while." Elizabeth checked herself. She wondered how much she should share with this girl. She reasoned that they'd probably never meet again. "Who knows?" she offered. "I might go there today."

Ellie shot her a wise glance. It looked out of place on her face. "Ah, I see. On a magical mystery tour, are you?"

"Not exactly." Perhaps it wouldn't hurt for Elizabeth to tell a tiny bit of her story. She looked squarely into Ellie's face and announced, "I'm waiting for the seventh train. I'm going wherever that goes."

The girl looked around the café for the departure board. She checked the display, mouthing numbers as she counted down the list of trains and destinations. "Err… that's Ipswich, I think, isn't it?"

Maybe she could have some fun. Elizabeth lowered her voice in an attempt to raise the drama. "Perhaps. If it turns up on time." And then, with an attempt at added mystery: "I've learnt that you can't put your trust in timetables."

Ellie's wide eyes blinked back at Elizabeth. Subtlety didn't work on her. She didn't have enough of it inside herself to be able to recognise it on the outside. It's the same with those rare individuals who are truly honest. They are the easiest people to deceive because they have no lies in them to recognise the ones that others tell most of the time. Or, in the words of the philosopher: "It takes one to know one." Ellie wasn't one. Instead of trying to figure out the motive behind Elizabeth's words, she decided to sidestep them altogether. "There I go being nosey again," she said dismissively.

"It's OK." It really wasn't OK. Elizabeth had opened a door that had been shut for a long time. Now that it was open, she could feel a breath of fresh air and was reluctant to close it again. She waited for an invitation to say more. She didn't have to wait long.

"You don't mind me talking to you, do you?" asked Ellie.

"No, I don't think so."

"I'm not being funny or anything, but you looked like the only normal person in this flippin' place." It wasn't clear whether this was a compliment or an insult. Elizabeth decided to take it as neither. It was merely a statement of fact. "I mean, it's all just part of the adventure for me. Look…" Ellie lifted the neatly piled objects off the paper bag and then re-scattered them noisily back across the table. She opened the bag and took out a small, colourful book decorated with facsimile passport stamps from exotic locations. "I bought this travel journal in the shop down there. Lush, isn't it? Look…" She flicked through the pages like a child with a new colouring book. "It's got a pouch for your tickets, and these pockets are for photos, and…" She noticed that her enthusiasm was not being matched by Elizabeth's expression. Ellie closed the journal and slipped it back into its paper bag. "Sorry. I do talk a lot, don't I? I don't mean to."

"It's OK." Elizabeth sensed the girl's awkwardness. "Honestly, it's fine."

Ellie chose to believe it, gave herself a little slap on the wrist again and let out a giggle of relief. "You're probably thinking: 'What a gobby, flippin' mare! Why did she have to sit at my table?' I mean, everyone tells me all the time: 'Ellie, do you ever shut the flip up?!' I even talk in my sleep, apparently."

Despite herself and her wish to maintain an aura of mystery, Elizabeth chuckled. "You do surprise me."

"Straight up! And the worst thing is that it's impossible to flippin' lie when you talk in your sleep. Did you know that?"

Elizabeth's scanned her memory banks, trying to recall whether anyone had ever told her that she talked in her sleep. Fortunately, she didn't think they had.

"It's true. I used to share a bedroom with my sister and she would say things like…" At this point Ellie sat up straight, as if that were the correct posture for big sisters. She put on a grown-up, deep voice: "'Ellie, Ellie – did you make out with Adam Healey behind the swing park?' And I'd be like totally fast asleep so I just had to tell her the honest, flippin' truth."

"And did you?" asked Elizabeth.

"Yeah, but we only did it once. Oops! There I go again. TMI." And then, just to clarify, Ellie added: "That means: Too Much Information."

Elizabeth was a tiny bit hurt by the girl's need to explain the common parlance to her. "Yes, I know what it means. I'm not *that* old."

Ellie apologised profusely. "Don't listen to me. I'm just excited, that's all."

Before she could take it back, Elizabeth found her hand reaching out to pat the back of Ellie's hand. It happened instinctively; she hadn't meant to do it, and she was surprised at her unexpected familiarity with a stranger. It was something she strongly avoided. It felt oddly natural but she pulled her hand away regardless. Ellie was sipping her coffee with noisy slurps. Under the table her feet were unconsciously tapping time to whatever up-beat earworm was currently playing through her head. Elizabeth could hear the faint drumming of Cuban heels on laminate flooring. 'There was no harm in the girl,' she thought to herself. Surely there was no need to be so guarded. Why would she want to squash this youthful bundle of exuberance that had plonked itself in front of her? She must have had a bit of that herself – once. When Elizabeth spoke again it was a little softer. "It's not a bad thing to be excited at your age."

"It's not a bad thing at any age, is it?"

"Quite right." Ellie's words had undone a few rivets in Elizabeth's armour. She started again a little tentatively. "Actually... I haven't had a proper conversation with another human being for ages. It makes a nice change, really."

"Oh, yeah?" Ellie was curious. "Have you been away then?'

"I've been everywhere and nowhere." It was clear that there was a lot more to be said. Elizabeth tried to say it. "I could tell you about it if..."

The mobile phone sprang to life again inside Ellie's bag. "Oh, for flip's sake! Sorry about this. So rude!" She rummaged around for the phone, checked the number, and swiped the screen. "Hi, Katy... I'm at the station now... Well, I don't know yet. If I need the number I'll text you... She just phoned... Yeah, I know." A snort of a laugh exploded from her lips. "No way!... Message it to me later... Yes, I'll be fine... Yes, I promise. Can't talk now, gotta go... Okay, laters... Promise! Okay, bye. Bye. BYE!" Ellie looked at the phone, tutted at the empty screen, and put it back in her bag. "Speak of the devil. That's the big sister I was telling you about." She tutted again even louder. "Honestly. How flippin' old do they think I am? They reckon I'm still a little girl." Looking at the ribbons in her shoes and the hearts all over her suitcase, Elizabeth could see the little girl in her too. "Anyway," Ellie continued, "you were just about to tell me where you've been and where you're going."

*The next train to depart from platform two will be
the twelve-twenty-nine service to Stansted Airport,
calling at Audley End and Stansted Airport only.
Platform two for the next train to Stansted Airport.*

In a moment of carelessness, Elizabeth forgot herself. "Three," she said.

Ellie corrected her. "No, I think they said platform two."

The man with the hat heard this and glanced sharply from one woman to the other. He wrote two words in his notebook and underlined them three times.

It was a sloppy mistake. Elizabeth knew that she had committed herself to an explanation. She was clearly useless at trying to be mysterious, no matter how much she'd love to be. She sat up straight in her chair. "I mean, that's the third train to depart since I've been here. Four more to go." She breathed a sigh of relief.

Confusion played on Ellie's face. "I'm not with you, babes."

The man with the hat closed his notebook and moved behind the women's table, checking the departure board over their heads. Elizabeth neither saw nor sensed him at first. Her focus was on how she would explain herself to Ellie. She decided to just say it. If the girl wasn't interested or didn't believe her, no harm done. If she was interested, for whatever reason, then she'd play it by ear. "Like I said, I'm waiting for the seventh train. That was the third train, so there's four more to go. When the seventh one comes, I'll be getting on it." She paused. "That's all," she decided. At least, for now.

29

"O – K." As Ellie visibly tried to formulate the next question in her mind, her eyes darted upwards, over Elizabeth's head. She frowned at what she saw while Elizabeth twisted herself round to see what had caused this sudden consternation. The man with the hat was right behind her, smiling that over-confident smile of his.

"Excuse me, ladies," he said. "Did they just say Stansted Airport?"

"Yeah, they did." Ellie's response was as confident as his smile. "So, if you've got a plane to catch, you'd better get a wriggle on."

"Right. Thanks." The man with the hat turned on his heels and went back to his table. He put his feet back up on the spare chair and opened his notebook. The two women were watching him intently. He acknowledged them with a nod, then went back to his scribbling.

Ellie lowered her voice, but not enough for the man not to hear what she said. "Well, that's just weird."

The man gave himself a knowing little smile, his eyes focused on the notebook. Elizabeth was still staring at him. She could feel a tightening of the nerves in her stomach but chose to ignore the sensation as best she could. Train stations were full of oddballs, in her experience. She rubbed her stomach unconsciously, as if she were trying to stroke away her nerves, and turned back to Ellie. "Obviously, he doesn't have a plane to catch."

"No," said Ellie. "Not him – *you*." She tutted as if it was obvious. "What do you mean, 'the seventh train'?"

Elizabeth picked up her coffee and swirled the last few, cold dregs around the bottom of the cup. She wished now that she'd bought another one, even if it was decaf. Her mouth was dry. "What the hell," she said. "I was going to tell you I was a hotel inspector, travelling incognito."

Ellie's face lit up. "Ooh, like that woman on the telly? My mum watches her every week and actually flippin' cries when some minging B&B gets four stars." She snorted with pleasure. "Is that what you do? Point out the pubes in the shower and all that?"

"No, I'm afraid not." Elizabeth had no idea what the girl was talking about. It was a long time since she'd watched any TV, and it really didn't sound like her sort of show anyway.

"Aw, that's a shame." Ellie looked genuinely disappointed. "I'd quite like that job, I reckon."

Elizabeth continued. "Or I could have told you that I'm an undercover journalist."

"Shut up!" Ellie was totally attentive now. Her hands grabbed the edge of the table as if she were trying very hard to keep herself from taking off into the air.

This was fun. Elizabeth was beginning to enjoy the game. "I might be exposing British Rail security in the light of increased terror threats."

"Really?!" gasped Ellie.

"Who knows?"

"Well," continued Ellie in a confidential tone, "My mate Chelsea's boyfriend says there's no film in the security cameras. Do you report that kind of stuff?"

Elizabeth tried hard not to laugh in Ellie's face. "I'm sure I would, if it were true, of course."

"But it *is* true, look..." Ellie stood up and glanced around the café, searching for a security camera. She spotted one on the wall just inside the door, strolled over as casually as she could manage, and stared straight into the lens. Without the slightest hint of self-consciousness, she proceeded to pull an absurdly silly face, then another, then another. Most of the customers in the café had seen Ellie's bizarre little display but pretended perfectly – in that very British manner – that nothing unusual had just happened at all. The only person who visibly reacted was a little boy, maybe three or four years old, who was sat with his mother at a table near the door. He clapped his hands with glee and proceeded to pull some pretty impressive faces of his own.

"Stop that, Harry," scolded the little boy's mother, loud enough for the whole café to hear. "It's not nice. People will think there's something wrong with you." She said it to the boy, who blissfully ignored her, but she had aimed the words at Ellie. The rebuke drifted straight past the girl, having no visible effect whatsoever.

Ellie turned back towards Elizabeth, shrugged her shoulders, and made her way back to the table. "See?" she said, sitting herself down triumphantly. "Nothing flippin' happens. And those were some of my best faces."

"Very impressive," admitted Elizabeth, "but I'm not a journalist, I'm afraid. Sorry to disappoint you."

The female announcer with the perfect voice was temporarily replaced by an older man with a not-so-perfect voice:

This is a customer announcement. We would like to remind Greater Anglia customers that CCTV cameras are in use throughout the station for your own safety and security. Thank you.'

The two women stared at each other, open-mouthed. The mother of the little boy tutted, throwing a smug look in Ellie's direction. The little boy just sucked loudly on a thick, chocolate milkshake.

"Flippin' hell!" cried Ellie, mortified. "Did I do that? Do you think they were talking to me?"

Elizabeth shrugged. "They're talking to all of us and none of us."

Ellie folded her arms and frowned. "I always thought Chelsea's boyfriend was a big, fat liar. He's got a monobrow." She brushed herself down as if she'd just been in a scuffle and settled back into her chair to regather her thoughts. "Anyway," she said, as if nothing had happened, "if you're not a hotel inspector or an undercover journalist, who are you?"

Elizabeth paused for a moment to think seriously before answering this disarmingly direct question. Now she really did wish she had bought another drink. "I tell you what," she proposed. "If you go and fetch me a coffee, I'll tell you all about it. Deal?"

"Deal." Ellie rose from her chair, delighted at the offer. She fished around in her bag and pulled out a round purse decorated with a fluffy, smiling, ginger cat.

"Here, here," Elizabeth put out a hand to stop her. "Let me give you the money." She opened her bag to look for her own purse.

"No way," Ellie flicked away the offer of payment with her hand. "A good story's always worth paying for. What can I get you?"

"Just a black coffee, please," replied Elizabeth. "The smallest size they've got."

"No probs. Watch my stuff for me," and Ellie skipped to the counter with surprising lightness, considering her chunky, Cuban-heeled shoes.

Chapter Three:
Chalk Farm Underground

The first journey began on a Wednesday morning at eight-forty-two; one long month before I had reluctantly offered a spare chair to Ellie at Cambridge station.

They say that January is the peak time for suicides. Perhaps it's the inevitable come-down after Christmas; an anti-climax for most people after all those parties and family gatherings and presents. For some, it might be the absence of those things. And then there's the crushing sense of failure from fresh gym memberships unused, and cigarettes smoked after quitting for three days. Divorce rates peak too, apparently. And debt, of course, after all those unnecessary gifts bought by people who couldn't afford them for people who didn't really want them in the first place. Luckily, I didn't have to suffer that one last Christmas. Or maybe it's just that the British weather in January is always worse than everyone expects it to be.

That first morning in North West London, the cold breeze was bitter and the sky was as grey as the pavements. The number thirty-one bus was crammed full of people. I had managed to get myself a seat, squashed in at the back on the long bench between a large, beer-sweaty man and the emergency exit. I remember thinking to myself, 'Someone stinking of beer already, and it's not even nine o'clock!' I've never been a big drinker myself; apart from parties, weddings, that sort of thing. Maybe that's why that particular thought sticks in my memory, and why the smell of alcohol in the morning disgusts me so much.

When the bus reached my stop, I didn't get up. It was partly because I was wedged in, tired, and feeling a little bit vulnerable. I didn't want to say 'excuse me' and tread on toes all the way to the door, so I did an odd thing for me and just sat there. At first there was a tiny thrill of excitement. I always got off at the stop before Finchley Road – never, ever the stop after – but that first thrill was brief. I made a point of being at work five minutes early every day. My deliberate punctuality was one of the few things I was actually proud of. This way I would be three minutes early instead of five, as long as I walked fast. 'No harm done,' I thought. The bus stops were pretty close together so I wouldn't have to walk far. But then another odd thing happened. I didn't get off at the next stop either, or the one after that. Now I would definitely be late and it disturbed me. I hated that more than the creeping feeling of insecurity that was twisting the nerves in my chest. I felt sick.

Then I remember thinking: 'If I'm going to get in trouble for being late, I might as well go the whole hog.' This flimsy reasoning satisfied me to begin with and the nerves subsided a little, despite the fact that I had never done anything like this before. I settled down in my seat, as comfortably as I could and decided that I would get off the bus at nine o'clock – wherever I happened to be at the time. I'm not sure what I thought I was doing, but there it is.

The electronic display board inside the bus said eight-fifty-one as it edged down the inside of the traffic at Swiss

Cottage. The roads were thick with crawling cars and vans and buses, stopping and starting and stopping in a kind of hypnotic procession. Bicycles and motorbikes wove a dangerous dance in and out of the traffic lines, and all of it stank of petrol and rubber.

'Two more stops,' I thought. 'I'll go two more stops and then get off.' But that was where the beer-sweaty man left the bus, so I decided to enjoy the extra personal space for a couple more stops. By the time I got off the bus it was nine-o-four and I found myself at Chalk Farm tube station. Time was slipping away from me and I was feeling uneasy about this strange, new situation.

A fat rain began to fall. I checked inside my bag for my purple, folding umbrella, but it wasn't in there. I ran through everything I'd done that morning and cursed myself for leaving it behind on the kitchen table. Why had I taken it out of my bag? It was only to check that my purse was in there. But my purse was always in my bag, in that little zipped pocket inside. I didn't need to check, so why did I do it that particular morning? That umbrella had been in my bag for six months, all through a hot summer and an unseasonably dry autumn, but now, when I actually needed it, it was sitting on the kitchen table, dry and useless. I was late for work, several stops from being where I should have been, and now I was cold and wet.

I'm not usually one for metaphors, but sometimes it really is just one little straw that breaks the camel's back. An innocuous little incident that sits so heavy on top of a thousand others that it brings a whole world tumbling down. I used to work with a quiet woman called Esther who left her husband because he put an empty milk carton back in the fridge. That's what she said. But it wasn't *that* carton – that carton was almost nothing – it was the hundred other cartons that lined up behind it in an invisible chain of disappointment. And every link in that chain, every empty milk carton, conspired to carry all the infringements forward together until it hit that marriage like a tidal wave of frustration. That's what I thought, anyway. I never mentioned my theory to Esther. Perhaps she understood already. If she didn't, it was too late by then to say anything.

It was only a little bit of rain. It was only a forgotten umbrella, but finding that it wasn't where it should be – another thing that made my life seem so pathetic – caused a pressure to build up inside me until it was strong enough to break the fragile walls of my composure. A string of images, thoughts, moments, surged through my mind in quick succession: every pointless job, empty relationship, useless possession, absent friend, disappointing holiday… none of them were huge, traumatic episodes in my life, but all of them piled together added up to a mountain of futility that I no longer had the strength or desire to climb. At least, not on that particular morning when I was late for work in the rain without an umbrella.

I didn't scream or tear out my hair. I didn't even swear under my breath. Instead, I walked calmly and deliberately into Chalk Farm tube station, touched my Oyster card to the ticket barrier, and waited patiently for the next lift to take me underground. As I waited, I remembered a story I'd once heard about a famous eighteenth-century suicide. The woman in question had left a note. It simply read: "All this buttoning and unbuttoning." That was it. I understood exactly how she felt. It was all just too much bloody effort.

On the Northbound platform, the digital display said two minutes until the next train was due to arrive. It didn't matter where it was going; the timing was perfect. I walked to the far end of the platform, where the train would be moving fastest when it came out of the tunnel, and took my place.

So often, in films and plays and novels, the perpetrator of a suicide is heroic, even glamorous; someone who is just too delicate or too good for this dirty world. Or a tragic victim of some unfair circumstance that makes the ultimate, devastating sacrifice. I felt none of those things. In fact, I felt very little, which was remarkably comforting.

It was the nothingness that made it all so reassuring. I did wonder, just briefly, if I should go home and plan it all properly – leave a note, make sure the fridge was empty, put my best dress on, and then come back to the station. Maybe I should send a letter to my mother in the care home. That wouldn't make any difference. My mother couldn't even remember that she had a daughter anymore. The Alzheimer's had her from the inside out. Besides, anyone who might care about me at all would find out sooner or later. I remember gripping the handle of my handbag with my right hand. It was the strongest feeling I had at the time. Perhaps because it was something physical, something quantifiable. Inside, in the purse that I'd checked for in the flat that morning, was a piece of credit-card shaped plastic containing all the information that anyone needed to know in order to identify me. It was my driving licence: name, address and date of birth.

There was even a photograph. I remember being glad that the picture had been taken a few years earlier when I was half a stone lighter. Ridiculous, now that I think about it. What did it matter?

There were still a fair number of passengers scattered along the platform. Maybe they were late for work like me, or perhaps they weren't due to start at nine like I should have done. Some were reading books and newspapers or staring at smartphones. Some were gazing idly at billboards selling lifestyles I didn't want or couldn't afford if I did. I looked at all the people as if they were one, long, worm-shaped entity. I wondered if these were the last human beings I would ever see on this earth. I was glad they were strangers. That way I wouldn't have to say goodbye, or even say anything at all. Still I was calm inside. Still I felt nothing. All the sounds and sights and smells of the Northbound platform swirled around outside of me, but nothing could make its way inside. It was like watching a movie or being in a dream; not part of it at all, just watching. I was numb. It all felt remarkably easy. I hadn't expected it to feel like that.

The rumble of the oncoming train grew louder and louder and louder in the tunnel, the noise rattling down the tracks and into the belly of the station, the train breathing dust and discarded rubbish ahead of itself as it came. The digital sign flashed 'Train Approaching' and so I counted: 'One, two, three…' I moved a step closer to the edge of the platform, well over the yellow danger lines that warned 'Mind the Gap.' I edged another inch closer as the rumble grew into a roar, filling my ears as I felt the blast of filthy air belching out of the tunnel. 'Four, five, six, seven…'

I remember the crash of sound. It was like someone had thrown a switch; like someone just turned up the lights and the volume all at once in a crescendo of colour and noise. All of my senses suddenly launched into danger mode, overriding the numbness in spite of myself. My ears, my eyes, my instincts sprang back to life and I was thrown backwards off my feet by the sheer power of it all as the train pulled onto the platform and came to a halt with a screech of brakes.

The train doors opened with a 'whoosh' and a 'clunk.' A young man that had been leaning against the wall nearby was now standing over me as I lay dazed on the dusty platform. "Are you alright, lady?" he said.

The man had headphones in his ears and pulled one of them out as he spoke. I could hear that annoying, hissy beat of some music I didn't recognise, and didn't care to. The first thing I did was search for my bag. It was still over my shoulder. I snapped back into myself and desperately fought to regain my usual composure. I managed it enough to answer him. "Yes, thank you. I'm fine," I said.

"You fell over," explained the young man, as if I hadn't noticed. He put out a hand to help me up. I took it and got to my feet. I wasn't hurt but I wanted to cry. I really did. But I stopped myself. Inside I was screaming, but "Sorry" was all I could manage to say out loud. The young man shrugged. "No worries," he said, popping his dangling headphones back into his ears. He jumped on the train just before the doors slammed shut, and then he was gone. So was everybody else.

I was alone on the platform for a couple of minutes, I guess. It was hard to estimate how long it was. I breathed out into the grimy underground air. That's when I noticed a dull pain in my left hip. I remember rubbing it to check that it was nothing serious. It must have got bruised when I fell over. And then I realised that the numbness was gone. I could feel again. The pain reminded me in a strangely neutral, non-judgemental sort of way. It's hard to explain. A hot tear rolled slowly down my cheek and I let it sit there for a minute, feeling it turn cold on my face, then I wiped it away with the back of my hand. The truth is, I didn't know what I was supposed to do next.

A couple of other passengers appeared halfway down the platform; two older women jabbering loudly about what line joins to what and debating the quickest way to Earls Court. I brushed a bit of floor dust from my coat and sat down on one of the empty metal benches. I watched as another passenger entered, and another, and another, then watched some more as the next train arrived, filled itself up with people like a hungry snake, then moved out to slither its way through the city. I wondered where everyone was going. They all looked so sure. I wasn't sure about anything anymore.

I made my way up and out of the station before the next train arrived on the Northbound platform. The fat, dirty rain was still falling outside and it stung my eyes. I crossed the road and tucked myself into the doorway of a small, empty shop to let, pressing myself against the padlocked glass door. Inside I could see a pile of discarded, crumpled newspapers and a doormat full of junk mail. At the back of the shop was a large, abandoned wall mirror. I caught my reflection in it; a shadowy reflection, turned grey by the sky behind me and the darkness inside the shop. I looked like a stranger trapped in some old photograph. I looked like anybody else. What would it take to look different?

Above the mirror at the back of the shop was a plain, round wall clock, obviously cheap enough to be left behind by the previous occupants. The clock said it was almost quarter past nine. I took my mobile phone out of my bag to check the time. It was correct. The clock in the shop was still working. I'd only been in the tube station for about ten minutes. How was that possible? I turned away from my reflection to face the street. The rain was beginning to ease and the morning was creeping on. The phone was still in my hand and I stared at it, trying to work out what to do. I thought maybe I should call work. It wasn't like me to be so late. They might wonder where I was.

After a few deep breaths, I called the number. It was answered after two rings by Helen on reception. "Good morning, Burgess Pinkton." The loud, breezy manner of the voice on the other end of the phone was almost painful and I held it away from my ear just enough so that I could still hear.

"Hi," I said. I noticed that the tone of my voice was deeper than normal and I was speaking more slowly and carefully. Perhaps that's what happens after someone almost throws themselves under a train. How would I know? I tried to sound natural, but my voice wouldn't pull back up into its usual timbre. It was just as well. It might help with the call I had to make. "This is Elizabeth," I said. "Is Peter in the office yet?"

"No, sorry. He's called in to say he's gone straight to a meeting in Highgate. You OK, Liz?"

I hate to be called Liz. No-one but my father ever used that name, and not for a long time. I haven't seen him for years; not since I was ten years old. Helen on reception always called me Liz like she was my best buddy, but we hardly knew each other at all. I didn't bother to correct her now. There wasn't really any point. I'd only corrected her once before, when I felt bold after a couple of glasses of Prosecco at some office do in Covent Garden. It had made no difference whatsoever. "I'm not feeling too good," I said. This much was certainly true. Then I paused for a second, gathered my thoughts and added a lie: "I hardly slept all night. I think it must be a stomach bug or something." The first and most commonly used fake sick excuse that I could think of. I'd never believed anyone else when they used it, and I didn't really care if Helen believed me now. I coughed into the phone for affect.

"Oh dear," said Helen, with no attempt at sounding concerned at all. "Aren't you coming in today then?"

I gave a little sniff at that point, then added a croak to my voice for good measure, just like I'd heard other people do. "I don't think I'll be well enough to come in." I replied. "Could you let Peter know and tell him that I'll hopefully be well enough to be in tomorrow?"

"Sure, okay."

"I don't think there's anything urgent on my desk."

"No problem." Helen didn't care if there was. "I'll pass on the message. Bye, Liz." And then, as a postscript, she added flatly, "Take care," then hung up before I could have the satisfaction of doing so myself.

In all of the five years I'd worked for Burgess Pinkton, this was the first sickie I had ever pulled. I expected to feel some sense of guilt, but I didn't. They wouldn't miss me for one day. Peter would just have to fetch his own coffee and Helen could reply to his emails. It was easy enough. We're called 'Personal Assistants' rather than secretaries these days but it's just the same old stuff – type letters, fetch coffee, lie to the clients, and do it all yesterday. And all of us as disposable as plastic forks. 'No,' I thought, 'they wouldn't miss me for a week, never mind a day.' This was the tenth job I'd had in almost twenty years, and this one was no more interesting and had no greater opportunity for progression than the last, or the one before that, or any of them. All I had to show for this string of dead-end jobs was a box full of leaving cards filled with names of people I couldn't remember, shoved into the back of a cupboard that I never looked in anyway.

The morning stretched out before me. All I had to decide was what to do with it. I spotted one of those trendy little brown-sign coffee shops a few doors down the street. I would start in there. It would give me time to think. It was getting on for half-past-nine and the coffee shop was almost empty. The half-awake morning crowd would have made it to work by now and it was too early for tea break takeaways. I sat down at a table for four and heard myself let out a loud sigh as if it had come out of someone else's mouth. I felt conspicuous in my smart but boring work clothes, as if someone might notice that I was playing hooky and disapprove. If only I had something to read in my bag. There wasn't even a menu on the table for me to pretend to look at.

A couple of minutes later the waitress came over, her dark blue apron folded down at the top and tied low around her skinny hips. Her strategically-torn jeans revealed brown knees and the hint of a colourful tattoo peeked out from under her shirt sleeve, creeping down towards her wrist. I thought how liberating it must be to dress like that for work every day. I remember feeling suddenly very stiff in my own, sensible clothes.

The waitress shifted her weight from one leather-booted foot to the other, pencil poised above a slip of paper. "Hi there," she chirped. "What can I get you?"

"I'll have a black coffee, please." It was a habit. I could have had anything I liked that morning, but I always ask for black coffee in cafés. It's strange, now that I think about it. I always have milk when I make it at home. Maybe it's because I still don't know the difference between a Flat White and an Americano.

"Cool," said the waitress absently, when what she really meant was 'OK.' "Anything to eat?" she asked.

I realised then that I was ravenously hungry – another side-effect of failed suicide that I wasn't expecting. "Do you have any muffins?" I enquired.

The waitress reeled off the list without pausing for breath: "Blueberry, lemon and poppy seed, double choc-chip, banana, or orange and white chocolate."

It was an easy decision. "Blueberry please." That was my favourite.

"Cool," she said again, which was clearly her stock response. "I'll bring it over to your table when it's ready." I thanked her, and off she went.

And there I was. Entirely free with nowhere to be and no-one to notice me not being there. I watched the waitress bustling around on autopilot behind the counter, steam spewing around her from the coffee machine. I watched and wondered if she could tell that her newest customer had almost killed herself less than half an hour before; that she wouldn't be sitting here at all if she'd not been such a coward. Did it show on my face? Could she hear it in my voice? Could she tell I'd been crying? But the waitress wasn't looking at me. She was too busy putting coffee in a cup and a muffin on a plate. Both duly arrived at my table where I sugared and stirred the coffee then broke the blueberry muffin in half to eat the bottom of it first. That way I could save the best till last. Do I do that with everything? I hope so. That means that there are better things to come... Doesn't it?

I hunted around inside my bag for my new, little red diary. I always buy one every year in the first week of January. By then, all the shops have them on sale, like if you miss the first five days, you're not going to bother buying a diary for the other three-hundred-and-sixty. It always gave me a ridiculous sense of smugness to think of all those people who had paid twice as much as me because they just had to have a diary before the thirty-first of December. Stupid, really. Even more stupid because there was hardly anything at all written in last year's diary, just a handful of birthdays and a dentist's appointment. I found the new diary and opened the page at the right date. It was one of those 'week-to-view' diaries that only have four lines allotted for each day and a little ribbon bookmark attached to the spine. I found a pen at the bottom of my bag, blew some fluff off the nib, and wrote four questions with four answers on the blank page:

'Q: Did you mean to kill yourself today? A: I don't know.'

'Q: Why didn't you jump? A: I don't know.'

'Q: Do you want to go back? A: No, there's nothing there.'

'Q: Where do you want to go? A: Nowhere.'

I put my pen down on the table and looked at the words I had written until my coffee went cold. I kept it to four lines. It meant that particular day was filled up in the diary. I could have carried on and written in the next day's space, over the lines, even sideways, if I'd wanted to. But I didn't. I guess that tells you a lot about me. By the time I'd finished my unplanned breakfast, I had made a life-changing decision. I wasn't going to go back. I couldn't see a clear way forward yet, but I definitely, definitely wasn't going to go back. I put the diary and the pen back in my handbag. They're still there now.

On that cold, grey Wednesday morning at nine-fifty-two, I stepped out of the coffee shop in Chalk Farm and walked to the nearest bus stop. I got on the first bus that came along – the number twenty-seven to Turnham Green – counted seven stops and got off. Now I was on Hampstead Road but it felt like the doorway into another universe. The next bus that came along, five minutes later, was the number twenty-four to Pimlico. I counted seven more stops and got off; New Oxford Street. And that's how it all began.

A couple of times, after counting seven stops, I found that I was hungry or needed to find a toilet, or just felt like having a look around an unfamiliar location, and so that's what I did. But then I'd find another bus stop and get on the first bus to come along, wherever it was going, and repeat the whole thing again.

Twelve hours later, I was exhausted but exhilarated; happier than I'd felt in years, perhaps ever. It was very strange. After all that bus hopping, I was now on the South side of the river. Despite the thrill of playing truant and the freedom that came with solo travel without agenda, I was reluctant to continue the same way on night buses. I rarely even ventured out of my flat at night these days, not unless I really had to go somewhere. Besides, after checking the timetable at the last bus stop, I realised that I'd have to wait on a quiet, dark, unfamiliar street for almost half an hour before the next bus was due to come along. There was a local map on the side of the bus shelter and I examined it carefully to get my bearings. South of the river was like a foreign country to me. Then I made the second big decision of the day. Possibly even bigger than the first. This would not be merely a one-day fling. It would become a brand-new way of life.

With my handbag clutched a little tighter to my chest, I walked a few minutes down the road to Waterloo Station. There were still a lot of people in the main concourse, probably heading home after a night out or a very long day at work. I checked the big, digital departure board, which flashed and flicked as trains moved out to be replaced by others, and counted the columns of destinations and the times spread across it. I decided to use a different formula on the trains. Rushing to get on the first one might prove stressful and it wouldn't leave enough time to grab a coffee or something to eat or an opportunity to freshen up. This would have to be something I'd never done before; the beginning of a new chapter, and it would have to work for as long as possible. It came to me like a blinding light of inspiration; a 'hobo epiphany' is what I'd call it if I were a poet. The thought of it had a fabulous fall-out. It removed all the angst and trauma of that Wednesday morning and the close call in Chalk Farm Station. Suddenly everything was fine. It was a deliciously simple plan with rules that I could follow. I would wait for the seventh train. After four stops I would get off, and then, wherever I was, I would wait and get on the seventh train. And on and on.

Three loud chimes rang around Waterloo Station and a voice with perfect diction followed:

The next train to depart from platform three will be the ten-thirty-nine service to Guildford via Epsom. platform three for the next train to Guildford.

I stood alone in the middle of all the night-time passengers at Waterloo Station. I remember saying something out loud. It was quiet enough so that no-one else could hear, but firm enough that I could feel it. "One," I whispered.

Chapter Four:
The First Train to Brighton

The coffee was getting cold. Elizabeth hadn't spoken that many words in one go for weeks. Not out loud, anyway. All the way through her story – shortened and carefully censored in places – she had forgotten to take a sip of her coffee. She picked up the lukewarm cup and drained half of it in one gulp. Ellie was the first person to hear the edited highlights of Elizabeth's journey so far, and it was a relief to the storyteller and engrossing for the listener. She brushed over the events on the platform at Chalk Farm station by simply stating, 'I almost fell under a train.' That way Ellie could make whatever she wanted of that particular chapter. She didn't want to frighten the poor girl. At least, that's what Elizabeth had reasoned to herself. The fact was that she wasn't ready to tell anyone about what had really happened. It wasn't denial. She was ashamed of what she'd tried to do and the guilt was still raw.

The man with the hat was scribbling furiously in his little black notebook. Ellie had been sitting there the whole time, listening intently between sips of cappuccino. Now that the story had come to an end, she was perplexed. Her brow furrowed and her head tilted to one side, like a three-year old working out four-hundred-and-five times eight-four. "Say that last bit again," she urged.

Elizabeth put her coffee cup down on the table. "When I arrive at a new station, I get on the seventh train, count four stops then get off and wait for the seventh train from whichever new place I happen to end up at." She said it as if it were the most normal thing in the world.

"Seriously?" It still made no sense to Ellie.

Further explanation was offered with deliberate casualness. "Yep. Then I get on that train, count four stations, get off, wait for the seventh train, and so on and so on and so on."

Ellie sat back heavily in her chair, her expression a mix of confusion and awe. "No way," she said.

"I believe the correct response is, 'Yes way.'" Elizabeth sat back in her chair too. She was relaxing into her revelations as the burden of the story was lifting from her shoulders. "I suppose it is a bit unusual, isn't it?"

"Just a bit!" exclaimed Ellie a little too loudly.

Elizabeth shrugged. "It's exactly four weeks since I started doing this. I hadn't thought of that till just now." She paused to sip a bit more of the lukewarm coffee. It was becoming increasingly bitter as it cooled. "You'd think I'd be further away from London by now, but the trains keep criss-crossing back through the capital like it's compulsory, and so..."

"Whoa! Just hang on a minute." Ellie stuck out both hands as if she was trying to physically stop Elizabeth in her tracks. She needed to give the maths one more go. "Let me get this straight – so, every seventh train that comes along you get on and go seven stops..."

"Four stops." Elizabeth corrected politely, but it was important to be accurate.

"Okay, four stops. Then you get off, count the trains and get on the seventh one that comes along at that station, right?"

"You've got it."

Ellie paused, stroked her chin thoughtfully with the back of her hand, then asked: "But why?"

It was an innocent, honest question. It caused Elizabeth to pause and attempt to reply with equal honesty. It also caused the man with the hat to stop writing and watch instead. His eyes were keen and alert, his pen hovering above his notebook. The women were now too far into the story to notice, or even to feel his sticky vision on their skin. "Why?" Elizabeth echoed.

"Yeah!" Ellie rolled her eyes in exasperation. "Duh! Hasn't anyone ever asked you that question before?"

Elizabeth shook her head. "I've never told anyone about this before."

"Wow!" Ellie was astonished. "So, tell *me* then. Why are you getting on seventh trains and counting five or twelve or however many stops?"

"Four."

"Yeah, yeah. I've never been good with numbers."

As Elizabeth paused to consider her response, the man with the hat waited patiently, as did Ellie. When she began to speak again, he wrote down the exact words that came out of Elizabeth's mouth: "I'm doing it because I didn't like where I was and every train takes me four stops further away."

"Away from where?"

"Nowhere," admitted Elizabeth. She hadn't thought about this reply. It just fell out of her mouth before she had a chance to consider it.

This simple, one-word answer was not what Ellie was expecting at all. She thought it would be something more complex; more difficult to argue with. The man with the hat put his pen down and approached the table where the women sat, oblivious to what was going on around them. His words made them jump.

"Excuse me, ladies."

The politeness of the statement and the friendliness of the man's tone had the effect of snapping Elizabeth back into the world beyond her café table rather abruptly. She glared at him and resented the intrusion. The process of sharing a bit of herself with Ellie had been unexpectedly cathartic and Elizabeth was enjoying it. Her response to the man was curt. "Can we help you?"

"Yes, you can," The man stood a little too close to the table as he spoke. "Have you finished with the sugar?"

Ellie was never deliberately curt. She remembered her manners and smiled politely at the man with the hat. "Yes, I have. Thank you."

The man responded with too much gusto. He was trying too hard. "Great! Do you mind if I take it back?" and he put out an open hand that hung in the air between the two women. Elizabeth noticed how smooth and soft the skin looked on his palm. He had clearly never done a hard day's work in his life.

"No probs." Ellie picked up the little white sugar bowl. "Here you go."

The man with the hat took it with a nod of his head, but he didn't move away from the table straight way. Elizabeth felt increasingly uncomfortable but said nothing. 'If he's waiting for me to speak,' she thought, 'he's going to have a bloody long wait.' He just stood there, holding the bowl of sugar and smiling. "Terrible habit," he said finally.

"Right," said Ellie.

"Rots your teeth, you know," and his smile widened to display a few of his; a bit crooked along the bottom row, but bleached that Beverley Hills shade of white that's almost ultra-violet.

"I know it does," agreed Ellie. She flashed him back a smile of perfect ivory teeth inside a pink lipstick frame.

"And causes hyperactivity," the man added.

"Yeah, right." Ellie launched into an overexcited little dance in her chair, complete with jazz hands, just to prove his point. Dance performance complete, she threw the man an even wider grin then stuck out her chin as if to demand: 'Anything else?'

There wasn't anything else. "Great," concluded the man with the hat.

"Great," repeated Ellie. Elizabeth still said nothing.

Then the man with the hat took the little white bowl of sugar and went back to his seat. He placed the bowl down carefully and precisely in the middle of the table, opened up his notebook and began to write once more. The two women watched without even attempting to hide it. He could feel sticky eyes on him, like he always could, but he didn't look up from his writing. He was enjoying the attention. Ellie folded her arms and tutted loudly, a frown puckering her brow. "He's not even using the flippin' sugar," she said with disdain.

Elizabeth chose to forget the intrusion rather than delving too closely into what it might mean. Surely the man with the hat would be gone soon too. He must be waiting for a train. Why else would he be sitting in here? She could simply pretend he wasn't there at all. It was something she'd become very good at. She would pretend now to be a happy wanderer without a care in the world. "Not bad coffee for a railway station," she stated in her best casual manner. "I might just have time for another quick one before the seventh train comes... Maybe an espresso this time. Or I could be naughty and have a hot chocolate. What do you think?"

Ellie stopped her right there. "Whoa, whoa! Hang on a minute, babes. Do you mind if I ask...?" She wasn't quite sure what to ask. "I mean could you...? No, I don't get it." Ellie unconsciously began to nibble at her bottom lip as she tried harder to concentrate on what she wanted to say. Elizabeth found it extremely endearing. "Let me start again. So, you're going nowhere, right?"

Elizabeth nodded.

"On a train."

"On the *seventh* train, yes."

"But *where* are you going?"

"I told you. Nowhere." Elizabeth swirled the remains of her coffee around her cup and sipped a little, waiting for Ellie to catch up.

"But that doesn't make any sense." Ellie was trying her best to understand. She was brought up to respect her elders, and to believe that age equates to wisdom, but she felt compelled to explain a little logic to this seemingly intelligent older woman. "The thing is," she explained, "we all start from somewhere and we're all going somewhere. There's a beginning and then there's an end... at the end! That's the whole point of journeys, isn't it? That's what travelling is *for*." Ellie emphasised the last word because she really, genuinely believed it to be the truth.

It was obvious that Ellie was beginning to feel exasperated. Maybe Elizabeth had told her more than she should, but too much had been said to go back now. She was committed, but she didn't want to upset the girl. She'd started something and the desire to continue was too strong to stop now. Elizabeth reached out and touched Ellie's hand softly. "I'll let you into a little secret, Ellie." Her voice was as soft as her touch. "Travelling is just a way of not staying where you are." Neither of the women saw the man with the hat write down that particular nugget of wisdom in his notebook, but he scribbled it down keenly.

Ellie's frown returned and she wriggled in her chair. "No, no, that can't be right," she insisted. "Travelling is the only way to *get* somewhere... Isn't it?" She was starting to doubt her own logic.

Elizabeth still had hold of Ellie's hand and was looking, searching into the girl's eyes. She was beginning to grasp her own words for the first time and wanted to try and make Ellie understand too. It felt important. It was as if she had to test it out on someone else to find out if it was real. It didn't have to be Ellie, it could have been anyone, but she was the one who happened to be there at the right time. She was the one who asked. No-one else ever had. Elizabeth could have been talking to herself, but the overriding feeling was that she had to try and understand, to make sense of what she'd been doing for the last month, even if no-one else could grasp it. But if someone else could, it might change everything. She took a deep breath. "What if you never want to get somewhere? What if you can't stand where you are but you're too frightened to arrive anywhere else in case there's absolutely nothing

57

there either?" She searched more deeply into the eyes of her young companion.

The older woman's eyes had grown wider and wilder. Ellie squeezed Elizabeth's hand in an attempt to soothe her. She tried again to appeal to her logic. "But there's something everywhere," she maintained. "That's the whole point. The world is full of flippin' stuff, ain't it?"

Elizabeth let go of Ellie's hand. She wasn't sure how to make her understand. "There's too much *stuff*, in my opinion."

"Ha! Not enough stuff, I reckon." Ellie patted her suitcase. "I could probably squeeze another pair of shoes in there if I had to," although it didn't look like that was possible.

Perhaps the women were just too many miles apart. Elizabeth had jumped a lot of hurdles and crashed into a few brick walls to get to where she was now. She couldn't expect someone like this, with her whole life in front of her, to have got to the same place. She decided to back off for a while and give the girl a break. "Do you really think there's something everywhere? I mean, something worth travelling for?"

"Yeah, of course I flippin' do." Ellie sat up, re-enlivened. Like most people, she loved to be asked questions more than she loved asking them. "I mean, next year I want to go to Greece with my mate Sam, right? Not *Naxos*, though!"

"What's wrong with Naxos?"

Ellie held out a hand and looked away in mock horror. "Don't even go there – literally!" She shuddered then continued unabated. "Then after Greece I want to go to New York, then Prague, and after that, who knows? Like I said, the world is my lobster. If I didn't have to pay any rent then I wouldn't have to go to work and I could be doing stuff like this all the time. I would flippin' *love* that. I could spend the rest of my life just travelling." She fell back into her chair satisfied.

"What, like me, you mean?" The question hung in the air all by itself until the female announcer with the perfect voice suddenly boomed over the tannoy and into the station café:

The next train to arrive at platform three is the delayed twelve-thirty-seven service to Birmingham New Street, calling at Peterborough, Stamford, Oakham, Leicester, Nuneaton and Birmingham New Street. Platform three for the next service to Birmingham New Street.

"Four." Elizabeth didn't care who heard her now. She had outed herself in the middle of a café at Cambridge railway station. It was as good a place as any. Most people within earshot of their table probably heard but thought nothing of it, except for the man with the hat.

Ellie folded her arms and took a fresh look at Elizabeth. She narrowed her eyes as she did so, as if that would magically bring the woman into some kind of new focus. "So, that's train number four, right?"

"That's right." Elizabeth sipped a bit more of her increasingly cold, black coffee. Its bitterness had the welcoming effect of re-awakening her senses.

Ellie had finished her cappuccino. "Three more trains to go then," she said.

"Three more to go," confirmed Elizabeth.

When the man with the hat strolled straight up to their table again, for what appeared to be no better reason than before, Elizabeth was more relaxed. She had already bared herself and her usual, comfortable fear of strangers was subsiding. He touched his hat with overcooked politeness when he spoke: "Excuse me again, ladies. Sorry to disturb you."

This time Elizabeth replied first, with new-found confidence. "Well, hello again. Can we help you at all?"

"You don't happen to have the right time, by any chance?" he asked.

It was a general question, but the man was peering straight into Elizabeth's eyes from under the brim of his hat. She held the man's gaze, determined to win this impromptu staring contest. "No, sorry. I don't have a watch, look…" and she pulled up her sleeve to reveal a naked wrist. The man with the hat glanced down to confirm to himself it was true, then straight back up into Elizabeth's unwavering glare.

Ellie was oblivious to the psychological skirmish going on in front of her. She was much more practical. "Excuse me." The other two blinked together then turned towards the girl. "There's a flippin' mahoosive clock on the wall up there, look…" All heads turned to where she was pointing. Indeed, there was a large, round, metal-rimmed clock on display for all to see but for hardly anyone to look up from their mobile devices to notice. "I reckon that should be the right time," said Ellie, adding a gratuitous "Duh!" for good measure.

"Ahh," said the man with the hat. "How did I miss that enormous time-piece. It must be three feet across," which indeed it was. "Sorry to bother you both." And with that he touched his hat, gave Elizabeth a little wink, and went back to his table and to his notebook and pen.

Ellie watched him move back to his seat. Her head tilted over to one side and then back again as she tried to weigh the man up. "There's definitely something weird about him," she decided.

Elizabeth went back to her coffee and swirled the last few dregs around the bottom of the cup. "Do you think so?" she said.

"Yep. Definitely." Ellie rested her chin on her hand as she watched the man in the hat. He knew she was watching him but was very deliberately not looking back at her. "I know," Ellie decided, "I reckon he fancies you."

"Thank you very much!" Elizabeth didn't like that conclusion at all.

"No, no. I don't mean *that* would be weird. There's nothing wrong with you, babe, apart from the train thing – take your foot out of your flippin' mouth, Ellie!" She slapped herself around the face, much harder than she intended. "Ouch!" She rubbed her cheek better and continued. "No, it's not *you* I was talking about. I mean *him*. He just looks a bit weird to me, that's all."

Elizabeth nodded in agreement. "Like I said, there's a lot of it around."

"Anyway," Ellie wasn't easily deterred. "Forget about him. Go back to the seventh train thing. Are you sure this isn't a wind up? Because I'm really gullible, by the way."

This girl had amused Elizabeth a lot since she'd sat down. She'd forgotten how simply pleasant it could be. "You? Gullible? I am surprised."

61

"True story," admitted Ellie. "My mate Sophie once told me that thirsty spiders come out at night and drink the tears out the corner of your eyes. I slept with my head under the pillow for weeks. And that was only last year!"

"It's a wonder you didn't suffocate."

"Well, I thought about that. I made a little air tunnel under the pillow with my fingers before I went to sleep so that I could breathe. I'm not an idiot!"

Elizabeth had to laugh. It came out warmly so Ellie didn't take offence. "The spiders could have just crawled down the air tunnel," she offered.

"Oh, yeah!" The thought of it made the girl visibly shudder. "I obviously didn't think it through, did I? But it just goes to show how flippin' gullible I am, so if you're winding me up…"

"No, no, this isn't a wind up, I promise you. I know it's strange, but everything I've told you is true." Elizabeth's words grew more wistful as her mind travelled back to that first day in North West London. "It's like people who always have to put their left shoe on first, or stir their coffee anti-clockwise. It's become compulsive with me. I can't stop." She paused as if she wanted to hear herself say those words more clearly. "I don't know if I'll ever stop."

The last comment made Ellie sad. It showed in her eyes. "What about your family? They'll be worried about you."

Elizabeth shook her head. She hadn't covered that part of her story. Now wasn't the time to go into details. "My dad left when I was a little girl, and my mum's in a care home. She's got Alzheimer's now. I don't think she remembers who I am anymore." There was so much more to tell, but she wasn't ready. "I was an only child," she said, "Now I'm an only grown-up."

Ellie reached out and put her hand on Elizabeth's arm. She didn't know what to say, so she just said: "I'm sorry."

The kindness of Ellie's touch was warming to Elizabeth. It was beginning to thaw something in her that had grown cold in the last few weeks. "It was all just going nowhere," she continued. "One dead-end job after another going nowhere, one shallow relationship after another going nowhere. Now *I'm* going nowhere. But this time, for once, I'm in charge."

"That's unbe-flippin'-lievable." Ellie shook her head.

"Well, you did ask."

Ellie patted Elizabeth's arm gently. She didn't want her to feel alone. It was something she had never suffered herself and she knew that she was fortunate. It was something her mother never stopped reminding her about. "What about friends? You must have friends that will miss you?"

"I thought I did when I was your age." Elizabeth smiled, as if to reassure Ellie that it was okay. As if she had accepted her lot. "Listen, Ellie: Friends are like trees. In the springtime, they're full of leaves and colour, but as you reach the autumn, all the leaves begin to fall until you're left with just the few bare branches that you started with. It all gets very thin." She continued with a shrug. "The few friends I've got left are so busy standing still that I hardly ever see them these days. They wouldn't know if I was alive or dead."

Ellie let go of Elizabeth's arm in order to cradle her coffee cup with both hands. She looked down into the cup with genuine sympathy for her companion. "That's really sad," she said. "I hope that never happens to me." As she stared at the leftover foamy patterns around her cup, she thought about her own circle of friends. She'd known most of them since primary school. They'd grown up together from girls to women and they knew everything about each other – all the good, the bad, the breakthroughs, the humiliations – and all captured in an extensive selfie archive. She couldn't imagine any of her friends not being there for the rest of her life. Nobody can imagine that when they're young.

It dawned on Elizabeth then that she was in danger of crushing Ellie and her natural enthusiasm before she'd even had a chance to make either success or failure of her adult life. It had been flattering at first that a young girl, full of vibrancy and colour, would want to know anything about some tedious, forty-something with so little colour of her own. Had she just been pouring her own emptiness, her own lack of fulfilment, into someone else for her own relief? It occurred to her, with disgust, that maybe that was what she was doing, and she didn't want to do that to the girl. It wouldn't be fair. She forced out a smile and attempted to lighten her voice a shade. "I hope it never happens to you either, Ellie. I really do." She paused, then added: "I'm sure it won't."

Ellie's gaze had still not left the bottom of her coffee cup. Her hands were still clasping it as if seeking some kind of comfort; as if looking for evidence of some kind of hope for this stranger that she now cared about. She didn't know what to say. Elizabeth noticed and forced her tone to sound perkier than it had been since the beginning of her story. "You see?" she explained, "I should have told you that I was a hotel inspector. You'd have believed that, wouldn't you?"

"Well, I did when you said it." Ellie looked up to see if she could figure out whether this woman was being serious or not. It wasn't easy to tell.

"I was a travel writer last Tuesday," Elizabeth said. "I can be anything I like to anyone I meet because I'm only passing through, just like you. I'll be out of your life in three trains' time."

There was a pause while Ellie thought it over. Her hands relaxed and let go of the coffee. She rested her chin on her upturned palms. They felt warm from the cup. "I hope you don't mind me saying this, but you look so... so normal!"

"Thank you – I think." Elizabeth laughed. It made Ellie feel better. She leaned in towards the girl and motioned for her to lean in too. She spoke with confidentiality, as if she were sharing a delicious secret. "A couple of weeks ago I was an anonymous art collector at the Royal Academy."

"Shut up!" Ellie wasn't actually sure what the Royal Academy was, but it sounded impressive.

"I swear it's true." Elizabeth sat up and put on her best arty voice, speaking with her nose in the air. "Just look at the way the form mirrors the theme of urban decay through the medium of light..."

"Huh?"

"Precisely." Elizabeth went back to her own voice, happy that she was beginning to distract Ellie from her previous sadness. "It's all bullshit. It's just an act to stop people from noticing who you really are."

Ellie sat back and returned to her earlier enquiry with renewed interest. "So, who are you, really?"

It was another one of her killer, straight questions. It didn't faze Elizabeth. This time she was glad to be asked, even if she wasn't sure what the reply should be. "That's a good question. I don't know, is the honest answer. I'm not sure I'm brave enough to find out."

Ellie studied Elizabeth. She couldn't be sure what was true and what was not. "No, I still think you're winding me up. You'd have to be minted. I mean, how do you pay for the trains? They've just put all the fares up. And then you've got to pay for hotels and B&Bs. Don't tell me you only sleep on the trains. You look too..." She looked Elizabeth up and down trying to select the appropriate word. "...too *clean*."

It was nice to know that, despite her boring attire, and after all those dirty stations and train carriages, Elizabeth at least looked clean. "Thank you very much."

"Well you do. But you don't look rich – no offence or nothing."

None was taken. "I have my railcard – that saves me a bit."

"Yeah, but still..."

"I've always been a good girl. My mother taught me to put it all away for a rainy day. I waited and waited until I realised there was no big day coming, rain or shine. Now I can spend the rent money on whatever I like, but there's nothing I really want to buy. In any case," she lifted up her shopping bag to emphasise the point, "I'd have to carry it around with me, and then you realise that possessions just weigh you down in the end." Then, she deliberately put her bag down next to Ellie's overstuffed suitcase. The contrast was stark and undeniable. "Anyway, I reckon I've got enough savings tucked away in the bank to last another five years, if I'm careful."

"Then what?"

The next train to depart from platform two will be the twelve-forty-five direct service to London, Kings Cross, calling at London, Kings Cross only. Platform two.

Ellie sat bolt upright. "That's my train." She looked rather disappointed.

Elizabeth just said: "Five."

"I could wait for the next one, if you want." The girl didn't want to leave – not yet. This unexpected meeting had had a profound effect on her and she wanted to stay with it. She tried to think quickly. "It doesn't matter what time I get to Brighton," she offered. "I think there's another train to Kings Cross in half an hour."

Elizabeth wouldn't hear of it. She was a lone traveller and she'd already disrupted this girl's day, not to mention her peace of mind. She wanted to make it clear that she had to travel alone. That had always been the plan.

"I don't mind, honestly." Ellie's eyes pleaded for inclusion. "Anyway, you haven't finished telling me your story yet."

Elizabeth realised then that she'd said too much. It was time to change tack. "There's nothing more to tell. I'm just a traveller with a strange sense of humour. I can be anything you want me to be."

It wasn't working. Ellie wouldn't be put off easily. "Could I take your number then? Maybe we could keep in touch."

"Sorry. I don't have a phone anymore."

Despite the fact that it was now becoming a little irritating, Ellie had a stubborn quality that Elizabeth could admire. The girl persisted. "First of all: OMG!" She raised her eyes skywards in total disbelief. "I've never met anyone who didn't have a phone," she shook her head as if she were trying to dislodge the incredulity from her brain. "Second of all: would you like to take *my* number. There might be a phone box somewhere. You could go old school." She was thinking on her feet. "If the seventh train goes to Brighton we could meet up, you know, perhaps if you want to go for a coffee or…"

This kind of thing had never figured in her plans. Elizabeth was a solo traveller. "That's very sweet of you, Ellie, but you really wouldn't want someone like me tagging along. You're going somewhere."

"Are you on Facebook?"

"Good God, no!"

Ellie made one last desperate attempt: "Twitter?"

"No!" That was enough. It would just be a waste of time trying to reason with the girl. In any case, the longer they debated the matter, the greater the chance of Ellie missing the train to Brighton, and then what? Moving the coffee cups to one side, Elizabeth carefully piled up the girl's belongings and pushed them across the metal table towards Ellie. Hopefully, the gesture would be understood.

At last, Ellie could see that her attempts were futile. Her shoulders rose and fell in surrender. She stood up, scooped her things from the table into her shoulder bag, manoeuvred the suitcase into its ready-to-roll position, and got ready to roll, herself. She was just about to say goodbye when she thought twice. She fished the travel journal out of her bag, along with a black eyeliner pencil, scribbled her number down on a blank page, tore it out and put it in the middle of the table. She attempted to reach out one last time: "Look, here's my number just in case. It's been so amazing to meet you. I mean that. And I really, really hope that…"

The girl looked sad, concerned, fretful; so different from the girl who had breezed in looking for a spare chair. Elizabeth wished that she could give her back the last twenty minutes. She could, at least, try to salvage something; undo some of the damage she might have done to her innocence. "Listen, Ellie, don't take any notice of me. The world really is your *'lobster.'* It was the same for me at your age. I was just bored of where I was going and thought it would be fun to make up a story, that's all." Ellie still looked unsure. Elizabeth pressed on. "Didn't you say every traveller has a story?"

"Yeah, but…"

She didn't give her a chance to argue. "Mine was just not very interesting so I embellished it a little. I'm sorry. I didn't mean to make you feel bad."

"Yeah, but…"

"Just think of it as part of the adventure – something to write about in your travel journal."

The frown was beginning to drop from Ellie's face, just a little. "Yeah, okay. But what about the seventh train?"

Here was Elizabeth's chance to land the story right where she wanted to. She shook her head. "There is no seventh train."

Ellie's open face expressed surprise then confusion then revelation then surprise again in quick succession. "But you said… I mean… wait… No way!"

"Again, I believe the reply to that is – Yes way."

Any sadness and concern was lifted from Ellie's shoulders and she thumped the metal table with glee. The coffee cups on it rattled in response, and she just managed to catch her own before it bounced off the table and smashed onto the floor. "That's mental! I swallowed the whole flippin' thing. See what I mean? I told you I was gullible."

The girl that first walked into the café was back. Elizabeth couldn't be more pleased. "Yes, you did tell me. Sorry. I just couldn't resist."

Ellie snorted at herself and pulled another of her many, impressively silly faces. "Great story, though. Much better than being a boring old hotel inspector… Oh, wait – you're not one, are you? Because I didn't mean…"

"I promise you, I'm not a hotel inspector. And that's the honest truth. Now, go!" Elizabeth shooed at her as if she were an escaped goose. "You'll miss your train."

"Oh, yeah. Right." Ellie pulled up the handle of her suitcase and turned to leave with a little wave. Then she had a thought and spun back on her heels. "Hey, maybe on the train I could be a scientist going to a top-secret convention on human cloning?"

"That's the spirit."

"Or a talent scout for a male model agency." Ellie glanced over at the man with the hat. He felt her eyes on him, looked up and threw a wide grin at the girl. She shot him a wide grin in return, looked back at Elizabeth and shook her head. "Maybe not."

The time was ticking on and Elizabeth could hear train doors opening and closing in the distance. "Go! Have a good time in Brighton."

"I will. Oh, by the way, you never told me your name."

That was no accident. Elizabeth wasn't ready for that kind of intimacy. When a person has your name, they hold a piece of your identity. She pretended not to receive the request so that she didn't have to refuse it. "Quick, quick, Ellie. You'll miss your train!"

"Oops! Better dash. Take care." And with that, Ellie scampered to the door of the café with some difficulty as the big, heavy suitcase trundled behind and her Cuban heels clicked noisily on the laminate flooring. And then, just as she disappeared through the door and out onto the platform, she called back at Elizabeth: "The world is my lobster! Bye!"

The little boy at the table near the door clapped his hands with delight at Ellie's loud, comic farewell. His mother tutted again and took his milkshake away.

The piece of paper with the eyeliner scribble on it was still sitting in the centre of the table. Elizabeth picked it up, looked at the numbers and the little 'x' scrawled underneath, then tore it into four pieces and put it inside Ellie's discarded coffee cup.

The next train to depart from platform one will be the twelve-fifty-eight service to Norwich; calling at Brandon, Thetford, Attleborough and Norwich. Platform one for the next service to Norwich.

Elizabeth sat back in her chair and hoped that Ellie had made it safely on to her train. 'Six,' she said to herself. The door to the café opened and a young woman breezed in wheeling a large suitcase behind her. Just for a moment, Elizabeth thought that Ellie must be coming back. Perhaps she missed her train on purpose just so they could spend a bit more time together. But it wasn't Ellie. It was some other young woman off on some other adventure and her suitcase was grey and shiny. There were no brightly coloured hearts on it or anything. Elizabeth was glad there was only one more train to go before she could get out of the café. She felt a bit lonely all of a sudden.

The man with the hat was putting his notebook and pen back into the pocket of his jacket. He took his feet off the spare chair, picked it up, and walked over with it to Elizabeth's table. "Excuse me again," he said.

Despite their smoothness, the man's words smashed through Elizabeth's thoughts. She didn't feel quite as confident now that Ellie had gone. She decided to be polite but nothing more. Talking with the girl had been an unforeseen pleasure; a happy diversion. It had even made her think, which had come as a surprise, but she wasn't ready to open up again just yet. That would take a lot more time. "Yes, can I help you?" she replied.

The man's insistent courtesy overpowered Elizabeth's politeness. He was, again, standing far too close to the table, holding out a chair in her direction. "I thought you might want this back," he said.

Elizabeth glared at the chair and then back at him. "That's okay. You can keep it." She wished that the next announcement would ring out around the station right now. The last one had heralded only the sixth train. She refused to change her plans for this man. Thankfully, he turned and went back to his table. Elizabeth didn't want to look around. Instead, she stared intently at the departures board on the wall, wringing her hands together under the table in the hope that no-one would notice the anxiety that was creeping over her.

But the man with the hat did come back. He had only gone to his table to put down the chair and pick up the little white bowl of sugar. He returned with it in his hand. "Sugar?" he offered, holding it out with a grin.

What was he doing? What did he want? If it wasn't for the fact that the café was full of people and it was the middle of the day, Elizabeth would have grabbed her bags and run as fast as she could out of the station. As it was, she didn't want to make a scene and draw unnecessary attention to herself. She declined the sugar politely.

With surprising grace and economy of movement, the man with the hat put the sugar bowl down on the table and, without invitation, pulled up Ellie's vacated chair and sat himself down. "So, not waiting for anybody then?" he asked.

Plenty of people were still in the café. If he tried anything there were at least five other men in there that would probably come to her assistance. However, Elizabeth didn't want to draw any more attention to herself. Her hands were still twitching nervously under the table. She noticed this, forced her hands to stop, then folded her arms, trying her best to appear calm. "No, I'm not waiting for anybody. If that's any of your business."

"None of my business whatsoever." The man leant back in his chair, hanging an arm over the back of it and crossing one leg over the other. He looked relaxed, like he was enjoying himself. Elizabeth certainly wasn't. She could feel her neck getting hot. She groped around by her legs for her shopping bag, pulled it a little closer, then re-folded her arms back in front of her. Maybe if she ignored him he would take the hint and go away. What did he want? He was going to tell her, of course: "It's just that, I couldn't help overhearing you say that you were a hotel inspector," he said with a grin, "and I thought, 'what a coincidence, so am I.'"

Elizabeth shrugged in an attempt at nonchalance. "You must have heard wrong. I'm not a hotel inspector."

"What a coincidence," he said, "nor am I."

The heat from Elizabeth's neck had crept up the sides of her face and was burning her cheeks. It was like the man was circling her; a killer whale toying with a shoal of herring. She pulled herself up in her chair and placed her shopping bag on the table to form some kind of barrier between them. Still she didn't look at him. "I'm sorry to be rude but I'm really not interested. Now, if you don't mind…"

The man with the hat continued. "And then I heard you say you were an art dealer. Didn't we meet at the Royal Academy last month?"

He must have heard everything – the truth, the lies, everything. She would try and front it out. "I've never been to the Royal Academy."

The man tilted his head back and laughed. "Well, that *is* weird. Nor have I. This is getting spooky."

It was becoming much more than spooky for Elizabeth. It was nothing short of sinister. Enough was enough. She pulled the shopping bag towards her across the table, and shifted her weight to the edge of her chair. "Look, do you want something or do you just come to railway stations to intimidate women?"

The man with the hat stared straight into Elizabeth's face as if he were searching for something. He raised his eyebrows, as if he had just found it. "No," he said, "In actual fact, I come to railway stations to wait for trains."

"As do I. Now, if you don't mind…" And without finishing her sentence, Elizabeth got up from her chair and readied herself to leave. She would wait for the next train in the waiting room along the platform. Or maybe she would visit the ladies' toilets and stay there until the next announcement came. It must be audible in there. But she didn't have to wait that long. Before she'd taken her first step away from the table, the disembodied voice reached out of the tannoy:

The next train to depart from platform six will be the thirteen-o-nine service to Ipswich, calling at Dullingham, Newmarket, Kennett, Bury St Edmunds, Stowmarket and Ipswich. Platform six for the next service to Ipswich.

"Seven!" But the word hadn't come from Elizabeth's lips. She had made sure to count this one in her head so that the man wouldn't hear. She froze, looking down at him, relaxed and happy, sprawled in his chair. "What did you say?"

The man gazed back at Elizabeth. Not a hard stare, not penetrating anymore, but waiting for something; some kind of recognition. "I think you heard me." Elizabeth didn't know how to respond. This was turning out to be a most unusual day, and a most unusual café. The man with the hat stood up and checked in his pocket to make sure his notebook was safely there. "That's my train," he said. "Nice to meet you." He turned as if to leave, but did it slowly in the hope that Elizabeth would stop him. She did.

"Wait! Why did you say 'seven?'" she asked with some urgency.

The man shrugged playfully. "Just train counting. It's a little hobby of mine. Easier than spotting them. Far too much paperwork involved, and I wouldn't be seen dead in an anorak."

But Elizabeth was having none of it. The innocent little word, 'seven,' spoken by this stranger had alarmed her and she needed to know who he was. This was *her* journey; her *idea*. Why was he crashing into it? It didn't make any sense. "You were listening to our conversation, weren't you?"

"It's a public place. You take your chances or you take a little more care."

"Yes, you do." Elizabeth wasn't sure if she wanted to know any more. She was confused. She would take her chances and get out now. Her train was waiting. This time it was her that moved to leave.

Before she could get past the man, he moved in front of her, blocking the narrow path between the tables. "Why did *you* say 'six' and 'five' and 'four'?" he asked.

"That's none of your business." Elizabeth felt dizzy, like she was just about to fall over. She had to get to the train but her legs wobbled and she reached out for the table. He caught her by the arm and held her carefully until she found her feet again. She straightened herself up, pulled her arm away, and looked him squarely in the face. Her voice was quieter but more insistent. She didn't want anyone else to hear. "Why did you say 'seven'?"

The man slid his chair carefully under the table. He liked to leave things tidy. "For the same reason that you did, would be my guess."

"And what reason is that?" she asked.

He smiled a playful smile. "You didn't think you were the only one, did you?" He swung around with a flourish, breezed out of the café, turned left and walked to the far end of the platform where the train was waiting.

Elizabeth could feel her pulse racing. There were still a few minutes before the train was due to depart. She got out onto the platform feeling hot and flustered, but there was no sign of the man with the hat. The guard saw her and pressed the button to open the nearest door. She composed herself as she approached, slowed down her movements and thanked him politely.

There was only one other person in the carriage – a young man in what looked like gardener's overalls. She took a table seat by the window and breathed. She pulled her shopping bag onto her lap and checked around inside it. She'd left the novel on the table in the café.

Chapter Five:
The Seventh Train to Ipswich

It was warmer on the train than it had been at the station. Even the café had been chilly by comparison, what with its door constantly swinging open as travellers moved in and out with the trains. The thick, grey clouds had parted over Cambridge, and the slight heat of a weak winter sun was magnified through the train carriage windows. Its amplified light illuminated the plastic table in front of Elizabeth making it look bright and clean, but she was sure it wasn't really that clean at all. She brushed her hand across it two or three times to remove any crumbs or bits of loose dirt.

Elizabeth settled her handbag onto her lap, the strap still stretched firmly across her body, and rummaged around in the shopping bag that she'd balanced on the empty seat beside her. She was still looking for her book. She knew it wasn't there but checked anyway. It's like someone going back again and again to 'the last place you saw' your keys, your purse, your pen, as if some invisible thief had felt a sudden pang of remorse and put them back when you weren't looking. Everybody does it. Perhaps the god of literature would leave Elizabeth a new book today. She glanced around the carriage, but there was no literary gift to be seen; just the young man in his gardener's overalls a little further down the carriage, gazing out of the window at the passengers milling in and out of the platforms like laboratory rats.

It was a good opportunity to catch a nap. There should be plenty of time to rest between Cambridge and the fourth stop, so Elizabeth curled her fingers around the handles of her shopping bag and closed her eyes. The young man in the carriage looked harmless enough, but she always held tight to her bag when she had to sleep on the trains. She didn't always sleep on the trains. It depended where she was and how long it might take to get to the fourth station. Sometimes she found herself in some place that was sure to have a cheap bed and breakfast or hotel, just like Harlow Town, and she'd check herself in. Once she'd spent the night in a freezing cold waiting room in a station in the middle of nowhere. She couldn't remember what it was called, but she didn't like it. She hadn't been disturbed except by a fat, grey mouse chewing a discarded leaflet in the middle of the room with no fear of the strange woman lying on the bench nearby. Luckily, she wasn't afraid of mice. It was the sound of rodent teeth on paper that she didn't like. That and the freezing cold. Right now, she was tired enough to sleep right where she was. She closed her eyes and felt herself sinking into the seat as the recording of a different woman with a perfect voice echoed around the carriage.

Welcome aboard this Greater Anglia rail service to Ipswich, calling at Dullingham, Newmarket, Kennett, Bury St Edmunds, Stowmarket and Ipswich. Thank you for travelling with us today.

"Ah, the historic market town of Bury St Edmunds. That should be interesting."

Elizabeth opened her eyes and sat up with a start, gripping her bag a little tighter. In her dozing state, she hadn't been aware of anyone approaching and sitting down at her table. The recorded announcement had covered any other noise, or maybe he'd deliberately crept up on her while her eyes were shut. She glared, frowning at the man with the hat sitting directly opposite her at the table.

"Lovely day for it," he remarked, beaming broadly. Elizabeth couldn't tell if his grin was meant to be sinister or triumphant. It had the effect of being both at the same time. She said nothing; just turned her head to look out of the window. The man with the hat persisted. "I said: 'lovely day for it.'"

Elizabeth searched around the carriage for any kind of reassurance; some kind of security. The young man with the overalls was still gazing intently out of the window, deep in his own thoughts. Surely the two men didn't know each other. They couldn't look more different. That gave Elizabeth a little confidence. She turned back to look squarely into the face of the man with the hat. He was still wearing that nauseating smile. "Are you speaking to me?"

The man with the hat sat back in his seat, making himself a bit more comfortable. "I am indeed." He looked like someone who knew exactly where he was going and how he was going to get there.

"Great." said Elizabeth, with as much nonchalance as she could muster. She settled back in her seat too and turned her eyes back to the window and to the train guard who was checking his watch. She thought about jumping off the train while there was still time, but she couldn't – or rather, wouldn't. These were her rules. It was the only the thing she had any control over on this journey. It was seven trains, not eight, and she wasn't about to let this stranger force her to change her own rules. Whatever he said. Whatever he wanted.

"It *is* great, isn't it?" he said.

Elizabeth held her ground. "I was being sarcastic."

The man with the hat shrugged. "Doesn't matter to me." He took his little black notebook from one jacket pocket and a pen from another. He placed them on the table as if he were daring Elizabeth to ask about them. She didn't, but she couldn't help peeking sideways at them anyway. Who was this man? How long had he been following her? What did he know…? He didn't appear to have any luggage, so hopefully he wasn't going very far. She would do her best to ignore him. If that was possible. The man put his hand on top of the notebook; watching her, teasing her by his small, deliberate actions. "Here we are again," he said. "What a coincidence – or is it déja vu, perhaps?"

Despite her best conscious efforts to keep her eyes focused on the window, Elizabeth couldn't help glancing between the man and his notebook. Despite herself and all her instincts, she stayed in her seat and found herself drawn into the conversation. "I don't believe in déja vu," she said reluctantly. "And I don't believe we've ever been on a train together."

"Ah," said the man, raising an impeccably manicured finger in the air to make his point, "You would only know that if you'd been looking for me on all the other trains."

"What makes you think I'm looking for anybody?'

The man with the hat leaned forward in his seat and stroked his chin with his hand. It was perfectly smooth, as if he'd had a shave that morning. He smelt of sweet lemons. "That's an interesting question," he said. "At least the first part, anyway. What makes me think…?" He sat back in his seat again and raised his eyes to the ceiling, scanning the empty space above his head for an answer. "I suppose all sorts of things make me think – now that I think about it."

"That should keep you nice and busy." Elizabeth sensed an opportunity to cut short this unforeseen turn of events. "Now, if you don't mind, I'm trying to get some rest." As she settled back and closed her eyes, the perfect recorded voice repeated its message into the carriage for any passengers who hadn't heard it the first time:

Welcome aboard this Greater Anglia rail service to Ipswich, calling at Dullingham, Newmarket, Kennett, Bury St Edmunds, Stowmarket and Ipswich. Thank you for travelling with us today.

"There it is again," the man with the hat persevered. "Interesting. Bury St Edmunds. Do you find that interesting?"

The man hadn't miraculously disappeared. He wasn't a bad dream or a figment of Elizabeth's imagination. She opened her eyes again and gave him her best cold stare. "You're determined to have a conversation with me, aren't you?"

He waggled a finger at her. "Determined is a bit strong. I prefer hopeful. Much better word."

Elizabeth folded her arms tightly across her chest. Irritation was giving way to indignation. "I hate to burst your bubble, but too much hope tends to lead to disappointment. At least in my experience."

The man with the hat shook his head and dropped his smile. "That's a shame. Have you been there before? Maybe you know something I don't."

"Been where?"

"Bury St Edmunds."

"How do you know I'm going there today?" Elizabeth didn't like where this was heading.

"It's the fourth stop from where we got on. That *was* what they said, wasn't it?" The man with the hat turned in his seat and looked around the carriage. He called to the young man who was still gazing out of his window deep in thought. "Excuse me." He was obviously very deep in thought. The man called out a little louder. "Excuse me!"

The young man in the overalls looked around the carriage until he noticed the man with the hat leaning towards him. He pointed at himself and raised his eyebrows, as if to say: 'Who, me?'

The man with the hat nodded in confirmation. "Did you happen to catch the name of the fourth stop on that announcement?"

The young man frowned. He looked at Elizabeth and then back at the man. "Sorry?"

Elizabeth frowned even harder than the young man. "What did you say?"

The man with the hat cleared his throat in an over-dramatic fashion. "Wow! Am I speaking some foreign language?" He leaned in towards Elizabeth with one hand on his hip and a smug look on his face. "Actually, I do speak French and a smattering of Italian. However..." He stood up and addressed the whole carriage, as if speaking to some invisible, waiting audience. "I'll try again in

English." And then, with mock over-emphasis and a perfect Radio 4 voice: "What is the name of the fourth stop from Cambridge?!" He turned from Elizabeth to the young man and back again, arms outstretched, awaiting a response. His normal voice returned. "Well? That's where we're getting off, isn't it? Of course, it doesn't really matter where it is, as long as it's the fourth stop." He turned back to the young man. "So, what I'm asking is: did you catch the name of the fourth stop on the train announcement, my friend?"

The young man stood up to give his reply. He wasn't really sure if he was supposed to stand up, but it seemed appropriate at the time. He spoke deliberately and a little too loudly in response. He didn't mean to mimic this strange man with the hat and his pronunciation wasn't as good as his. There was a definite Northern accent. "Yes, I did catch the name of the fourth stop. It's Bury St Edmunds." Then he felt suddenly self-conscious and wondered why he was standing up. He sat back down swiftly.

The man with the hat gave a little salute. It was clearly an affectation of his. "Thank you very much, young man."

"You're welcome." The young man turned back to his window, but not to the thoughts he was having before he had been so curiously interrupted. Now he was listening to this odd stranger who was conducting himself and his fellow passengers like a package holiday tour guide, and this middle-aged woman who looked like she'd hardly been anywhere. He tried his best not to watch them, or to be seen watching them. He managed it part of the time.

The guard on the platform blew his whistle. Elizabeth was glad to be moving away from Cambridge and all the uninvited conversations that seemed to be haunting her today. She realised, however, that now she was stuck on the train with this man for at least one more stop before she could escape. She made a mental note of where the emergency button was, just in case. Or she could just move to another carriage. Maybe he'd follow her. It was the middle of the week in the middle of a winter's day. The rest of the carriages were probably just as empty as this one. At least here she had another passenger nearby that looked harmless yet strong enough to step in if the man with the hat made a move. Across the table, the man was looking out of his own window as the city streets and houses thinned to make way for flat, cold fields. She decided to ignore him… but she couldn't. The nerves were tightening in her stomach. "Were you listening to the whole of my conversation with the girl in the café?"

The man with the hat pretended everything was as normal as could be. He picked up his notebook and flicked through it absently as he spoke. "I wasn't listening on purpose. Not at first, anyway."

"Not at first? So, you hadn't seen me somewhere… else? Before the café?"

The man with the hat paused and genuinely tried to remember if he'd seen her before. He wrinkled his nose and shook his head. "No, I don't think so. But I heard you counting trains when I sat down." He grabbed the front of his hat and pulled it down so that he could peek at Elizabeth from under it. "Did you know you were counting out loud?"

All of Elizabeth's senses went into high alert. She was so used to being anonymous that she'd forgotten herself in that café. Like drivers on motorways who pick their noses with childlike abandon, forgetting the clear glass between them and the rest of the world. They might as well be sitting in the middle of Piccadilly Circus. "I didn't expect anyone to hear me," she said. "Why would they be listening?"

The young man in the overalls heard that and turned his head abruptly to the window. He hoped the woman hadn't seen him staring. The man with the hat relaxed and tilted his head back to study Elizabeth's reaction to his next statement. "Well, I *did* hear you… and I wondered if you were another one."

"Another what?" asked Elizabeth.

"Another one of us."

"What are you talking about?" she demanded. "Another one of who?"

The man pushed his hat back off his forehead and spread out his arms in a gesture of benevolent inclusion. "Another Seventh Trainer, of course."

Before Elizabeth could challenge this outrageous statement, the perfect voice came over the train's PA system. It was beautifully on cue; as if the spreading of the man's arms had conjured her up.

Welcome aboard this Greater Anglia rail service to Ipswich. For your safety and convenience, customers are advised to familiarise themselves with the safety instructions displayed inside the carriage. Thank you for travelling with us today.

The young man with the overalls got up from his seat. At first, Elizabeth was worried that he might be moving to another carriage and leaving her with this strange man, but he didn't. Instead he picked up a rucksack from the seat beside him and moved to the back of the carriage, two seats behind Elizabeth. He put his rucksack down and began to read the safety instructions from the printed poster on the wall. Elizabeth and the man with the hat watched him. He glanced over his shoulder, caught the man with the hat throwing him a friendly, little wave, then went back to reading the poster. He followed the words with his finger, trying very hard not to glance around again. He decided to be ready to move – just in case he was called to – but for now he had to familiarise himself with the safety instructions.

"He's a safety-conscious guy," said the man with the hat. "Very sensible these days," and he reached for an energy bar inside his jacket pocket and tore into the top of the paper wrapper. "Would you like a bite?"

Elizabeth couldn't work this man out. "No thanks," she said.

"Please yourself." The man took just a nibble from the top of the energy bar and chewed casually.

"I know I'm going to hate myself for asking..." Elizabeth felt committed to a question nevertheless, "but, what's a Seventh Trainer?"

The man with the hat snorted and a tiny bit of something that looked like a sesame seed escaped from his mouth. To Elizabeth's disgust, he picked it up from the table, put it back in his mouth and swallowed. "What's a Seventh Trainer?" he mimicked. "Oh, come on. You didn't think you were the only one, did you?"

If she understood him rightly, that's exactly what Elizabeth thought. She checked all the same. "I don't know what you mean."

"Sure you do." The man with the hat put his energy bar down on the table. A few more sesame seeds spilled out. This time, to Elizabeth's relief, he brushed them onto the floor. With both the crumbs and Elizabeth's feigned ignorance swept aside, he continued: "I'm thinking of jumping on a ferry and starting on the French trains, once I've run out of British ones, that is. What do you think?"

Elizabeth didn't reply. She just stared at the curious man with her mouth open.

"Well, have a think about it. The trains might be cheaper over there. Food might be better too. Let's face it, it couldn't be much worse." He picked up the energy bar again and tucked the wrapper neatly back round what was left. He put it in his pocket for later, looked at Elizabeth and raised his eyebrows as if to say: 'Well?'

She spoke carefully and loudly enough for the young man at the back of the carriage to hear and witness. "Who the hell are you? And bear in mind that all I have to do is push the emergency button and…"

"It's a handle these days," the man with the hat corrected.

Elizabeth remained focused. "I'm not kidding."

"Nor am I." The man with the hat shrugged. "It's not a button, and it hasn't been a cord for years, either. You should know that."

The young man in the overalls turned and leaned over the seat in front of him to make his voice more audible to his fellow travellers, and especially to Elizabeth. "He's right, you know."

"What?!" Elizabeth turned to see the young man's face leaning in towards her over the seat behind.

The young man straightened up and spoke with authority. "It *is* a handle, and there's a penalty for improper use. Says it here..." He pointed to the list of safety instructions on the wall.

In a whole month of train-hopping, Elizabeth had never found herself on a journey like this. She looked from one man to the other and back again, eyeing them with suspicion. "Do you two know each other?"

The man with the hat stroked his chin again thoughtfully and studied the young man's face. "No, I don't think so. Have we met, my friend?"

The young man moved forward until he was standing next to Elizabeth's table. He looked more closely at the man with the hat from a polite distance and shook his head. "No, I don't think so." He noticed then that Elizabeth was gripping her handbag and shifting her weight towards the window. "Are you alright, lady?"

"Yes, thank you." Elizabeth tried to sound strong and self-assured, but her words came out in a high-pitched squeak.

The young man straightened himself up to his full height – which wasn't nearly as much as the man with the hat – but remained firmly polite. "Is he bothering you?"

The man with the hat let out an involuntary spurt of laughter. The young man straightened himself up another inch. The man with the hat put up his hands in a friendly act of submission. "It's okay. Everything's fine. We're just fellow travellers passing the time." He put his hands back down and motioned instead to the empty seat beside him. "You're welcome to come and sit with us, if you like."

The young man declined. "Thanks, but I only like travelling forwards." He'd accepted the older man's submissive gesture and put his hands in his pockets, as if to say he wasn't going to fight him right now, but he was prepared to, if called upon. He turned to Elizabeth. "Unless you'd feel safer if I sat there?"

Just hearing the young man say it had been enough to reassure Elizabeth. He seemed genuine enough. His overalls were a little too large for him, and she could tell that underneath them he was slightly built and quite a bit shorter than the man with the hat, yet he was there, ready to come to her aid if she called on him. She was pleased about that. "I'm okay. Thank you."

"Right," he said. "I'm just back here if you need me." Then the young man took his hands out of his pockets and turned to the man with the hat. "No disrespect, mate," he said.

"None taken."

"I'm sure you're a gentleman." It was unnecessary to add that comment, but the young man was trying to be a gentleman himself.

The man with the hat appreciated the additional remark. "Thank you very much, young sir," and he flashed that little salute of his again.

All was now equal, and so the young man in the overalls turned and went back to his seat. From there he could keep an eye on the odd couple and listen to the unfolding, increasingly curious conversation without being rude.

The man with the hat continued, but with deliberately increased volume so that the young man wouldn't have to strain too hard to hear them over the sound of the train on the tracks. "Friendly guy," he said to nobody in particular.

Elizabeth felt safe enough to continue with her questions, now that she felt the young man had her back. She leaned forward to get the full attention of the man with the hat. "Who *are* you – seriously?"

The man shrugged, not intimidated in the least. "I'm just a fellow traveller."

"Of course you are. That's what you told him." Elizabeth didn't want to play games. "How much did you hear of our conversation in the café?"

"Just bits and pieces." The man with the hat flicked through the pages of his notebook, noticed Elizabeth's eyes focusing on it, then put it away in his pocket for later. He didn't put the pen away just yet; instead, he picked it up and twiddled it between his fingers as he spoke. "I do know that we're doing the same thing but for different reasons."

It was like pulling teeth without anaesthetic. Elizabeth's frustration was beginning to show in her voice. "Alright. You've got my attention. That's what you want, isn't it?"

"Come on," said the man with the hat, "who doesn't like a bit of attention?" The pen twiddling stopped, turned in the opposite direction, stopped and turned again in a lazy, hypnotic dance.

Elizabeth tore her gaze away from the pen and back to the man. "So, go ahead – tell me. I know you want to."

The man with the hat put the pen down on the table and leaned forward like an excited schoolboy. "I *do* want to tell you, actually. Is it that obvious?"

"Yes, it is."

The train lurched around a bend and the pen rolled across the table and onto the floor. Elizabeth bent down and picked it up. As she handed it back to the man, she noticed that the end was peppered with teeth marks. Was he a thinker? Or perhaps just a nervous traveller like her. He didn't look nervous. If anything, he looked completely in control. He took the pen and put it in his pocket. "It's just that I find the whole thing so fascinating."

Elizabeth leaned back and folded her arms, studying her uninvited companion. She'd had a month of almost total solitude, despite spending most of that time at railways stations, on trains, in streets, surrounded by plenty of other people. And just like the buses that started her on this peculiar journey, you wait for one human to talk to you and then three come along at once. "Go ahead. Enlighten me," she said.

The young man got up, grabbed his rucksack, and moved to the seat behind Elizabeth. The man with the hat watched, smiling. "Can you hear a bit better from there?"

The young man ignored the direct question and addressed Elizabeth instead. "I'm just letting you know that I'm here in case…" And then, not really knowing yet what the case might be, he added: "Just in case."

Elizabeth turned and smiled. She noticed, for the first time, how young this man looked. He must be in his early twenties. She was old enough to be his mother.

The man with the hat didn't want the focus taken away from him and the centre stage that he'd carefully cleared for his forthcoming revelations. "Now, where was I?" he insisted.

A little, unconscious click of his fingers above the table caused Elizabeth to turn her attention back to the man, albeit grudgingly. "You were just about to enlighten the whole carriage with your wisdom."

"So I was," said the man with the hat. "You see, I could be wrong, but I think you're doing the seventh train because you're frightened of reaching the end. I'm just going by what you said in the café back there."

"Okay." Elizabeth's mind began to whirr. This concise conclusion felt true, but she'd avoided coming to it herself. It sounded almost trite, when summed up like that. The man with the hat was waiting for some kind of confirmation, but she wasn't ready to give it to him. "Carry on," she said.

He was happy to. "My reason is different. I'm doing it because I'm in love with the middle. Same journey, different reasons. Fear versus love, in fact." He leaned back in his seat and put his hands behind his head, satisfied with how the whole thing was going.

Elizabeth wasn't ready to be analysed, not by anybody, and especially not by this stranger who wouldn't even take off his hat in polite company. "So, I'm frightened and you're in love – is that it?"

"If you like."

"No, I don't." In fact, Elizabeth was liking this less and less. More than that, she hated the fact that she was increasingly intrigued by what this man had to say for himself.

"Well, give yourself time to think about it." He leaned back in towards Elizabeth, put his elbows on the table and rested his chin gently on the palm of one hand. It made him look suddenly wistful and had the added effect of removing any previous signs of arrogance. "I've thought about it a lot," he continued, "and I've come to the conclusion that the opposite of love isn't hate, as most people seem to believe. It's actually *fear*." He leaned back in his seat again and looked out of the window, taking in the dark green of the passing fields. "I think about a lot of things on the trains."

"Obviously." Elizabeth tried her best to appear disinterested. She opened her handbag, with its strap still stretched across her body, and fished around in it. She then pretended that she couldn't find what she was looking for, lifted the strap over her head, and placed it on the seat next to her. It was the first time in days that she'd taken that strap from her shoulder or not had it in contact with her body. Even on the nights when she'd booked herself into a hotel, she'd slept with it under her pillow or tucked in beside her. There wasn't much in it, but her bank card – the portal to her life savings – was in there. It was only that thin, plastic rectangle that allowed her to keep moving on this journey. She was usually so careful about keeping it safe. Right now, she wasn't being so cautious. There was too much else to think about.

The man with the hat noticed Elizabeth putting her bag on the seat. It had drawn his attention away from the dark green fields and the country houses. He was a watcher and he always noticed things like that. He thought it might be important, but he didn't realise just how significant it was. "Anyway, you seemed unhappy about your reasons and I found that interesting," he said. "I'm happy about mine."

"Humph!" Elizabeth wasn't convinced. If he was such a happy wanderer, why was he bothering her? "That must be very nice for you." She said it with sarcasm, but the man with the hat was having none of it.

"Oh, it is."

"But it's not about reasons – it's about choice. And I don't know about you, but I have no choice."

The man with the hat exhaled with a snort. "Bullshit! There's always a choice."

"Oh, really? Tell me then, oh wise one." Elizabeth heard the words come out of her mouth and didn't like the venom that came attached to them. It was too late to take it back. Fortunately, the man with the hat barely registered it, or didn't care to.

"Okay," he said, "I'll tell you. But do you mind if I ask you a question first?"

"As long as you don't mind if I choose not to answer it."

"Aha!" The man with the hat clapped his hands as if he'd just pulled the words out of Elizabeth's mouth himself. "There you are, you see? Choice!"

"Very clever." She pushed a lock of stray hair back from her forehead and could feel that her face was getting hot.

Neither of them had noticed that the young man behind Elizabeth had moved forward in his seat, enjoying the verbal sparring going on at the table. He wished he could be clever like them and join in. 'Maybe when I get to their age,' he thought. He leaned in a little more and listened.

"Okay," said the man with the hat, "here's the question. And I'll make it an easy one for you."

"You're all heart."

The man with the hat swept his hands outwards across the table, as if he was clearing the way for his question. "How long have you been travelling like this?"

Elizabeth paused to leave space for him to be impressed. "Four weeks exactly to the day, if you must know."

He wasn't overly impressed. "No time at all, really."

She folded her arms, disappointed that she hadn't impressed him at all. "I suppose you've been doing this your whole life."

"No," he said, "that would be silly." He clasped his hands together, resting them on the table in front of him and looked straight into Elizabeth's eyes. It made him look now like he was conducting a job interview – and the candidate wasn't doing very well.

Elizabeth glanced through the gap between her seat and the neighbouring one towards the young man. He didn't see her. By now, he was listening so intently that the front of his head was resting on the back of Elizabeth's seat so that he could concentrate completely on the conversation in front of him. He suddenly became aware that he was being watched, flashed Elizabeth a nervous little smile, and sat back in his seat.

The man with the hat seemed oblivious to the whole little drama. "I've been on the trains almost three months." He waited for a gasp of awe, or perhaps some applause. Neither came. "You started on the buses, didn't you?"

"You *were* listening carefully at the café, weren't you?"

The man didn't pause to either confirm or deny it. "I did meet someone who started on the underground once." He took a sharp intake of breath. "That must have been depressing. Round and round, packed into all those noisy tubes under the streets. Mind you, I've been through London sixteen times, so far. Why do they all have to go back to London?" He stopped, and thought about it for a moment. Unseen by the other two, the young man did the same. "Stupid question, really. I guess all roads lead to Rome."

The young man behind Elizabeth looked puzzled at the last statement. She wasn't, but she didn't find his joke particularly funny. "Three months?" It was only just now sinking into Elizabeth's brain just what this man was saying.

"Yep. Three months to the day, actually. That's a coincidence, isn't it? Looks like we share an anniversary."

Elizabeth nodded her head thoughtfully, resigned now to the fact that she really wasn't the only one. It was a bit too much of a coincidence to be an accident.

The man with the hat relaxed into his story. "I haven't done all the stations yet. They don't all join up, you know. I'd have to cheat and switch to buses to cover some of the smaller ones and the tourist railways."

The green fields skimming past the windows had turned into villages and back into fields again. They must be getting close to the first station by now. Elizabeth had no idea what time it was. She'd deliberately left her watch on the very first train exactly four weeks ago.

The door slid open at the far end of the carriage and a ticket inspector breezed through, calling for 'tickets from Cambridge.' It was a welcome interruption for Elizabeth. She thought about all the journeys; all the tickets bought and railcards flashed; all the times she'd found herself crossing London again, just like this man said. For the first time, she felt like there was someone who might know how she felt – at least about the travelling. Someone she could compare herself to and perhaps learn about herself from. This unlikely stranger was holding up an imaginary mirror that she hadn't even realised she was searching for; a reflection that she needed to see. The carriage door opened and closed again. The ticket inspector's job was done.

When Elizabeth spoke again it was softer, more exposed. "How long do you think you can keep going?"

The man with the hat shrugged. "Who knows?" His voice softened too, responding to Elizabeth's new, warmer tone. "As long as possible, is the plan."

She nodded in recognition. "Until the money runs out."

"No, no," he said. "Until the *feeling* runs out," and he emphasised the word 'feeling' with his hands, lengthening the word as he spoke it. "I used to be a film director, you know."

This new piece of information took Elizabeth totally by surprise. The young man poked his head up from behind her seat, his eyebrows raised and his expression keenly curious. The man with the hat spotted him and gave a little wave. The young man waved back shyly. "You're a film director? Cool! I love movies."

"Excellent! Another film fan." He suddenly had them in the palm of his hand. "Yes, I direct, write, sometimes produce." Now he could tell them his story, because a storyteller was really what he was. "My name's Ray, by the way."

"I'm Barney." The young man raised his hand again in greeting.

"Nice to meet you, Barney." Ray tilted his head towards Elizabeth. "I didn't catch your name."

"I didn't throw it at you." Elizabeth was quietly startled and supremely satisfied at her ability to come back with a witticism so quickly.

"Very good," said Ray. "I like it."

Elizabeth liked it too. Like so many people, it was exceptionally rare for her to be able to pull out the perfect, slap-down response – clever, cutting and fitting, all at the same time. She made a mental note to remember it if anyone ever presumed to ask her name again when she didn't want to give it. She was pleased to finally know his name, though. It meant that, for now, she had a little more of him than he had of her. "So, tell me, Ray," she prodded, "Should we have heard of you?"

"Perhaps," said Ray. "I was fairly successful."

Chapter Six:
The First Train from Paddington

I always wanted to be in the movie business. Even as a boy, I'd go to the pictures with my little friends and fantasise about seeing my name up there in big letters on the screen. It's not because I was a conceited child – that came later – nor did I want to be the handsome hero in the close-up shots. No, I wanted to be the one behind the camera, pulling the strings like a puppet master. Perhaps it was early signs of megalomania. If it was, I'm over it now. Conceit is enough to be getting on with.

One Saturday afternoon, when I was not quite six years old, my father took me to see some spy-chasing, fast-car-driving action flick in one of the big cinemas on Leicester Square. I don't know how he managed to get me in because I was way too young to see a movie like that. I never thought to ask him, though my father always had a way of getting people into places they shouldn't be – but that's another story.

So, there I was, sitting in a red velour seat, little legs swinging two feet from the floor, face full of chocolate when, all of a sudden, a good guy shoots a bad guy and there's blood pouring down his shirt like a crimson waterfall. Well, I was absolutely horrified. I dropped my Maltesers and proceeded to scream my head off as little balls of chocolate rolled about all over the floor. You'd be surprised how much noise falling confectionery can make on raked seating. All that attention couldn't have been good for the cinema's admission policy, not to mention their licence, but I just kept on bawling. In fact, I didn't stop crying until my father had carried me out of the cinema to the Italian café on the corner and bought me a double cherry sundae and a large coke.

As I stuck my spoon into the icy goodness, dad began to explain, carefully but firmly, that what I had just seen on the big screen was not real. All of those people were just pretending to do what they were doing. It was called 'acting.' He went on to explain that what I had assumed to be blood was, in fact, tomato ketchup, and what usually happened was that the actor would eat it all up once the camera was switched off, probably with a large plate of chips. I was totally captivated. A whole new world had opened up for me and I pumped him with question after question:

"Are *all* the people in the films just pretending, daddy?"

"Yes."

"Even the bad guys?"

"Especially the bad guys."

"So, they don't really die when they get killed?"

"No."

"Are the people on TV real?"

"Some of them."

"Which ones are pretending?"

"Most of them. Especially the politicians."

I carried on with my interrogations until both the ice cream sundae and my father's patience had run out. My overpaid, overworked father usually had very little time for children, even quiet, well-behaved ones, which I certainly wasn't. This was ironic, really, because he was a producer of youth programmes for the BBC. That was the first and last time he ever took me to the pictures.

Later that same day, my mother came into my bedroom to let me know that supper was ready. She ran out shrieking and screaming for my father, and once he'd calmed her down and given her one of her little blue pills, he was able to explain that it was only tomato ketchup. Nobody had broken into the house and murdered her only child.

Two weeks later, for my sixth birthday, my doting mother bought me a brand new, top-of-the-range video camera. It was way too big for my clumsy, little hands, so I constructed my own tripod device from washing-up bottles and pieces of Lego. My precociousness knew no bounds, and so with the help of my new Panasonic M1 camcorder, mummy's little genius began his film career. I knew that I would be a success. It might sound arrogant, but I knew it because I worked hard at it every day until it happened, and that's what it takes. Of course, it also helps if your father is a producer at the BBC.

I've still got a VHS copy of the first short film I ever made – *The Beast of Buckinghamshire* – starring our compliant old retriever, Ferdinand, and my mother's fox fur jacket. I must dig it out some time… the video, not the fox fur. I'm totally anti animal products nowadays, with the exception of the occasional steak… and the odd bacon sandwich. It wasn't a bad start, and Ferdinand was a star in the making. He became my muse until I hit puberty and turned the camera on girls, along with a few boys on the way. Ahh, I do miss Ferdinand.

Fast forward a few years – insert grainy montage of teenage/young adult me doing stupid things, mostly half-naked – until we arrive at my early twenties relatively unscathed and with only one regrettable tattoo. Said body ink, incidentally, was so badly applied that I can no longer remember whether it's a bleeding heart or Darth Vader.

My first major hit was *The Hot Cheese Sonata*. I was twenty-three years old and my star was rising. Fabulous reviews, great box office, universal praise. It's the one where Mabel Heep plays the President of Botswana. And no, the casting wasn't my first choice, but her agent insisted that Ms Heep – which is what I always called her on set – wanted to stretch herself. We had all kinds of backlash on social media; people saying that only actual heads of state should be allowed to portray Presidents, that sort of thing, but La Heep won them all round in the end. It was a remarkably convincing performance. She walked off with a Golden Globe and two Oscar nominations: one each for Best Actor and Best Actress.

What everyone admired the most was the surprise ending. They all loved it, critics and audience alike, but I won't spoil it for you. However, that's where all the trouble started. Overnight I became the 'master of the ending' and I couldn't shake it off. Famous for it now, of course. So, the next movie got an even bigger budget. Hollywood producers couldn't chuck the cash at me quick enough. I gave them what they wanted, because I didn't know any better at the time, but I swore that *Hot Cheese Sonata 2: It Ain't Over Till The Feta Lady Sings'* would be my final master ending. It won two BAFTAs and a Golden Rooster, but I wasn't happy. It nearly killed me. The money helped a bit, of course.

The one thing I learned about winning awards is that you get about six months to sell any damn thing you like, no matter how awful it is, as you ride the wave of success. In retrospect, I do think the Zumba DVD was a mistake, despite the stellar cast, but you can't win them all.

After six months, things got quiet again and I had a chance to gather my thoughts and plan where I was going next. LA is nice and all that, but it was never really my style. I can't stand the exercise. Besides, I've always been a London boy at heart. So, I bought myself a loft apartment on the trendier side of Paddington – yes, there is one, by the way – covered a whole wall in my study with blackboard paint, and purchased six boxes of chalks in a range of colours. I always like to work big.

I was still getting plenty of offers of work, particularly from the big studios. They all had stacks of screenplays that were almost right but not quite. All they needed was a 'great director who could fix the ending and turn it into a megabuck-grossing blockbuster.' That's exactly what Sony Pictures said. A little bit hyperbolic, I know, but the others weren't much different. Universal even offered me two million to remake 'Joan of Arc – with a twist!' A tiny bit of me did consider that one for about half an hour, but I recovered my sanity and turned it down, just like all the others. I didn't want to be the master of the ending anymore; not at any price. That's much easier to stick to when your bank account is bulging, by the way. I'm not an idiot.

What people couldn't understand was that I genuinely hated reaching the end and the come down that inevitably followed. It hurt. It left a sour taste in my mouth. It was like a new death every time and I was sinking into a deep depression. At first I tried to explain my feelings to the producers and the studio bosses, even to a couple of brave screenwriters that contacted me direct. How they got my private number, I'll never bloody know, but I admired their balls for calling. The trouble was, nobody understood what the hell I was talking about.

I lost a couple of weeks to alcohol. Honestly, I have no idea what happened in that time. All I know is that I got through fifteen bottles of brandy, twelve litres of vodka, four cases of champagne, and a bottle of pear and elderflower pressé. I have no idea what that last one was about. Perhaps I had a visitor that day. Or perhaps I thought it was food because every other dietary substance that had been in my fridge at the beginning of that two weeks was still there at the end, only now it was either green or black or a little bit furry.

It was my next-door neighbour, Maroon, that found me. She told me that when she walked in, I was sitting cross-legged in the open dishwasher, fast asleep with my head on the Sicilian marble worktop, with a BBC oven glove on my head. Apparently, after emptying a half carton of rancid orange juice over my face, she managed to wake me up, at which point I proceeded to complain that I hadn't finished washing my trousers. It took several cups of espresso to bring me back to some kind of coherence, by which time I was able to thank my neighbour profusely for saving my life; if not from certain alcohol poisoning, then from dishwasher-induced hypothermia. She said she wouldn't have come round at all except that I had *The*

Final Countdown by Europe playing very loud on repeat and it was driving her insane. Luckily, I had given her a spare key for emergencies when I moved in to the block. I guess I must have foreseen such circumstances. I knew myself better than I thought. Maroon is an actress from soap land. This overpriced apartment block is full of them. I think I promised her a part in my next movie in return for her samarital act. It's the least she deserves.

Once I'd enjoyed a much-needed shower and taken a car full of empties to the bottle bank, I felt renewed. No, it was more than that – I felt reborn. Something had been set free; something had been purged along with all the alcohol I threw up after the hot shower. So, I sat down in my study with my ergonomic office chair facing the big, blank, blackboard wall, and began to write my masterpiece – the one that would be studied in future film degrees all over the world; the one that would make me an auteur; the one that would break the boundaries of film-making forever. I was so imbued with it that I got it out in less than a week. The blackboard was full, and so was every scrap of paper in my apartment. That kind of inspiration only happens once in a lifetime.

It was pure genius, if I say so myself. No beginning and absolutely, definitely, defiantly, no ending. Just a middle that went on for eight and a half hours. And that was just going to be part one of a whole sequence of films; the same story running on and on and growing and changing, but never, ever ending. It completely took me over and I wrote like I'd never written before… or since, come to think of it.

As soon as it was all typed up, printed and bound, I sent the manuscript to every producer and director and film studio that I knew, which was pretty much all of them. Then I sat back in my comfiest designer armchair and waited for the awe and the offers to come back…

…They all hated it. They just didn't get it at all. One by one the answers came back, some sent direct to me with polite responses like: 'Not sure if the market is ready for this right now. What else have you got?' Some came indirectly via friends and acquaintances with not-so-polite responses like: 'What?! Is he nuts?' or 'Has this guy been taking too much of the sneezy powder?!' and other such slurs on my character, not to mention my ability to write a screenplay.

Well, I was absolutely devastated. I almost lost another two weeks to alcohol, but I was so depressed I couldn't be bothered to go to the off-licence. I didn't eat for three days, which actually meant I was able to lose that five pounds that I'd been trying to drop for months, so it wasn't all bad. I wouldn't recommend it as a lifestyle diet, although several Hollywood actresses seem to have beaten me to it. I won't name names. You know who they are.

Those three days of starvation did more than reduce my waistline, though. I've never been one for self-denial, so when the hunger pangs grew too great, I ordered a large pizza, two portions of onion rings and a selection of dips. As I sat guzzling the pepperoni perfection, melted mozzarella dribbling down my chin, I gazed at the blackboard and saw the light. Not literally, of course. I hate it when people misuse that word. I *figuratively* saw the light. The over-sized Anglepoise had been on the whole time.

It became clear that the so-called 'professionals', the Hollywood producers, the big studios, the money men

– because they are all men, pretty much – would never have the vision to understand what I was trying to do. Too much money and power has a way of stifling creativity with remarkable efficiency. The more you have, the more you're scared to lose it. That wasn't going to happen to me. I decided to skip the big guys and go straight for the real people – the audience; those who had less to lose. I would make a shorter, four-hour version of my movie and put it on, at my own expense, at an independent film festival in Bristol. I thought, 'OK, we'll let the audience decide.'

...They hated it too. I'd totally overestimated my audience. It wasn't the characters or the plot they hated; not even the music. In fact, the soundtrack album sold millions and is still available to download online. No, they just couldn't handle not having a beginning or an end. I had to concede that Aristotle was wrong. Very over-rated Greek, in my opinion.

I had clearly forgotten why people went to the movies. All those years working in the film industry, boy to man, and it was obvious that I'd disregarded a very important fact: Most people don't go to the movies to be entertained or, God forbid, educated. No. They simply go in order to escape from their own, miserable lives of drudgery. The masses don't want to know the truth about their situation – anything but. They simply want to get lost for a couple of hours in a world that's not real because the real world is full of so much shit these days. In any case, there's plenty of fake reality on TV. You don't even have to get up off the sofa.

You see, in real life there's no ending or beginning. It's all a process. We're right in the middle of life all the bloody time. It's not complicated. We make it complicated and then run away from what we've created, just like Frankenstein and his monster – and the original with Boris Karloff is still the best, in my opinion, and I don't care what anyone else says. The fact is, movies, TV, the internet, it all just gives us somewhere to escape to.

That realisation almost led to bottle-hitting time again, but I decided against that. Instead I invited Maroon over to talk about it. My head was reeling and I was in a hurry to sort this out. She happened to be the human being in closest proximity at the time. I also figured that, even if she had no idea what I was talking about, she'd be pleasant to look at while I talked. It started off quite well. Our conversation went something like this:

MAROON: But you have to have an ending. Every story has to have an ending, doesn't it?

ME: Why?

MAROON: Because everything ends; everything dies eventually, whether we like it or not.

ME: Does it?

MAROON: Of course it does, silly. We just don't want to admit it. That's what I'm trying to escape from. That's what we're all trying to escape from. That's why I take my vitamins every day.

ME: You're wasting your money.

MAROON: Listen sweetie, nobody wants to die. None of us want to get to the end, but we all have to one day. There's no point denying it.

ME: But the end is just a new beginning that leads to another wonderful middle. Can't you see it?

But she didn't see it. Nobody did. Despite a positive start, Maroon was just like everybody else. So, we drank a bottle and a half of brandy and went to bed. We've been avoiding each other ever since.

And there we are. I was a visionary with no-one to talk to. I thought I was being totally original and that my message would be welcomed by the world; that they'd all been waiting for it – but I was wrong. No, that's not entirely true. The message was right, I was sure of that, but the vehicle had stalled. Something had to change. 'Show, don't tell.' that's what we writers are supposed to do, so I decided that must be the way. Instead of trying to tell people the truth about the middle, I would live it instead; lead by example until others got the hang of it. Live the process instead of pretending, fabricating, lying about the fact that life has a beginning, a middle, and an end. It just bloody doesn't. We are all energy and energy cannot be destroyed. It just turns into something else eventually.

That same afternoon I left my warm, safe, expensive flat with nothing in my pockets except a notebook, a pen and a platinum credit card. I'm not an idiot! I walked down the road to Paddington station and got on the seventh train. I didn't even check to see where it was going.

Chapter Seven:
Dullingham Station

The sky had begun to darken and a sharp, spiky rain was stabbing at the windows of the train carriage. "It's started to rain," said Ray, as if he hadn't said anything else before that.

Barney and Elizabeth had been listening to Ray's incredible story. Barney, in particular, had been hanging on every word. He had punctuated the tale with regular cries of 'Wow!' and 'Amazing!' while Elizabeth had said nothing. Finally, she decided to comment. "So, I guess that makes you just another dreamer. The trains are full of them."

Ray sat back in his seat and traced some slow-falling droplets of rain on the window with his finger. "What a shame," he said, in a melancholy kind of way. "I thought you were one of us, but you're just another one of them."

Elizabeth took the comment as an insult. "Thank you very much," she said.

The affront hadn't been deliberate. Ray stopped playing with the rain and attempted to make eye contact with the injured party. "I didn't mean to be insulting, honestly. It's just harder than I thought to make people understand."

"Well," said Elizabeth, "Thank you for the stimulating story. It certainly helped to pass the time." Then, she thought about it and said: "And if you really are who you say you are, I loved *The Hot Cheese Sonata*. I used to have it on DVD. Now, if you'll excuse me…" and she fished around in her bag once more for the book that she knew for certain was still on the table in the café at Cambridge station.

She had underestimated Ray's tenacity – and his love of his own voice, for that matter. He continued to try and explain to her where she was going wrong and how much insight he might have. "At least now you know how that young girl might have felt."

Still, Elizabeth hunted for the lost book in vain. She dismissed Ray's unwanted comment without looking up at him. "She'll be fine. She's young."

"You made her question her reasons," he explained

"I don't think so," said Elizabeth dismissively.

"Just like I questioned yours." Ray made himself comfortable. His certainty was settling in again. "People find that rude – I'm not sure why – but I apologise if you did," although he really didn't look that sorry. "It's just that you looked so unhappy about your situation."

Elizabeth bristled at the assumption and stared now straight back at Ray; book search abandoned and arms freshly folded in defiance. "The state of my happiness is not your concern."

Ray shrugged. His skin was thicker than Elizabeth's stare. He was, after all, a veteran of the bad review, thanks mostly to all the Rotten Tomato ratings for his film about the middle. "Maybe you're right," he said," but most of the others I've met have been grateful to meet a fellow traveller on this peculiar journey." He turned back to the window and started to play with the rain streaks again. It was a clear invitation for Elizabeth to press him on such a provocative sentence.

"You keep talking about the others. What others?"

Ray looked at Elizabeth sideways, weighing up how much to say and how to say it. He tested the water. "Like I said, we're not the only ones." Elizabeth was doing her best to remain expressionless, so Ray sat back in his seat and decided to say whatever he liked. "At first, I thought it was my own brilliant idea. However, there's clearly nothing new under the sun."

Elizabeth rolled her eyes. "Really? Clichés now?"

"I would never use a cliché in a million years!"

"Very funny."

"I don't get it," said Barney under his breath. The other two didn't hear him. Even if they had, they probably wouldn't have responded. They were too embroiled in their game of verbal tennis.

"It's true, though," said Ray. "Just like all clichés." He waited for affirmation. None came. Not from Elizabeth, because she didn't want to, and not from Barney, because he still had no idea what they were talking about. Ray continued regardless. "Like I said, I thought I was being totally original at first. The day I walked into Paddington station, I truly believed that nobody had been ingenious enough or brave enough to do what I was about to do. But I got on that seventh train, counted four stops, got on the next seventh train, and so on and so on, and here I am."

"Just like that," said Elizabeth.

Ray leaned forward to speak unapologetically straight into Elizabeth's face. He punctuated each word with a carefully timed tap on the table for emphasis. "Just – like – you." Then he relaxed and sat back satisfied. "But much as I love it, it does get a little lonely sometimes, don't you think?" He raised his eyebrows to extend the question from his mouth up to his forehead.

"Ah, is that what this is all about?" Elizabeth suddenly felt vulnerable and very female, in the worst kind of way. She tried to make herself look slightly bigger and tougher as she sat in her seat. "I see where this is going," she said. "I'm not looking for a male travelling companion, thank you very much."

Ray smiled. It wasn't the kind of smile Elizabeth was expecting. It was neither lecherous nor intimidating. Instead it was simply amused, which she found rather disappointing. "Sorry," said Ray. "Lovely though you are, I didn't offer."

"Well, just so we're clear."

"We are," said Ray.

"Good," said Elizabeth, although a bit of her didn't mean it. She suddenly felt plain and frumpy and remembered now why she had made such an effort to be anonymous; not just since she had started this whole business, but pretty much all her life. She thought about just getting up and moving to another carriage. Nothing was stopping her. She was sure that Barney would intervene if Ray tried to do anything. He was still sitting right behind her and it was obvious that he'd been listening to everything. Yes, that's what she would do. This journey was becoming far too uncomfortable. She didn't want to think about the things this stranger was putting in her head. For all she knew, he was making it all up like she had with the girl in the café. Perhaps *he* was a hotel inspector or art collector, or something far more boring that needed a ridiculous story to make up for it. Elizabeth started to gather herself and her belongings. She was just about to say 'excuse me' and get up from her seat when Ray stopped her. Not physically, but with more of his story. To Elizabeth's own frustration, it wasn't politeness that kept her in her seat but cold, hard curiosity.

"It was three weeks before I met the first one," said Ray, without any attempt at seeking permission to continue. "I was going through London for the fourth time and there he was on the eight-fifteen to Folkestone, pretending to be a wind-sock salesman from Crewe." He smiled at Elizabeth then glanced at Barney, waiting for some kind of reaction to his opening comment. Nothing came back. He decided his companions had little to no sense of humour, but continued all the same. "We got talking, as you do, and he told me that I was the third Seventh Trainer he'd met. And it's odd because we all seem to have started within the last three months. Isn't that fascinating?" Again, Ray waited for some kind of reaction; astonishment perhaps, or a tiny bit of reverence. Still nothing. He shrugged and continued. "So far, we've all met on trains during our journeys. You're the first one I've found sitting in a station café. Must be a sign, I reckon."

Now Elizabeth felt she must comment. "I don't believe in signs," she said.

"What a coincidence," said Ray. "Neither do I."

The woman with the perfect voice was next to comment, her voice over-riding everyone else's:

We will shortly be arriving at Dullingham; Dullingham is your next station stop. Please remember to take all of your personal belongings when leaving the train.

"One," said Ray, with boldness.

"One," said Elizabeth, with equal defiance.

"Two," said Barney, quietly and with no real confidence at all.

Elizabeth and Ray froze and stared at each other. She felt like she'd been thrust into one of his ridiculous movies. It would be laughable if it wasn't so alarming. "What did he say?" she asked.

"I said TWO!" said Barney, his voice rising to a shout.

"He said two," echoed Elizabeth. She put her head in her hands in disbelief. "Oh, my God, he said – two!" When she lifted her head again, she could see the glee plastered all over Ray's face. He looked elated. She wasn't sure whether to laugh or cry, so decided to do neither. Instead, she just sat there feeling numb.

Ray clapped his hands. "There you are, you see? I told you. And here's another one. Ta-da!" and he held out an open hand as if he were introducing a new act into this circus of a journey. It wouldn't have surprised Elizabeth at all if Barney had suddenly jumped into the aisle and started juggling with flaming torches. He didn't, of course. He just sat there looking sheepish.

The train began to slow down, and the high-pitched screech of brakes replaced the steady rhythm of wheels over tracks. A cluster of houses and then a few more replaced fields and trees through the windows, and the woman with the perfect voice returned.

This station is Dullingham. Please remember to collect all of your personal belongings when leaving the train. Thank you for travelling with us today.

As the disembodied announcement echoed around the carriage, Ray and Elizabeth had both turned to stare at their new companion. Barney threw them both an awkward smile. "Is it alright if I come and sit with you now?" he asked.

Ray motioned to the empty seat beside him. "It was just a matter of time," he said sagely.

The young man picked up his baggage and moved awkwardly down the aisle. He shoved his rucksack a little too roughly under the table, accidentally knocked Elizabeth on the ankle and apologised. "Do you mind if I sit next to you? I don't like going backwards."

"I tell you what," said Elizabeth, "Why don't you both sit on this side? I'm starting to care less and less which direction I'm going in."

After much shuffling, re-arranging and apologising, the new positions were taken up and Barney settled down next to Ray. He turned to study the man carefully. "You're a Seventh Trainer," he said, as if it needed saying out loud.

"That's right," confirmed Ray.

Barney then turned his attention to his other new companion. "And so are you," he said.

"I don't believe it." She glanced from one man to the other and then back again, clutching her handbag close to her chest. "You *do* know each other, don't you?"

The two men ignored Elizabeth's suspicions. They focussed on each other instead. "How long have you been doing it?" asked Barney.

"Three months."

"Me too!" said Barney, and the men spontaneously high-fived each other, much to Elizabeth's distaste. She hated the way these Americanisms had crept across the pond. The two men continued like they were on some trainspotting speed date.

"Where did you start out?" asked Ray.

"Actually, I got on the first train at Crewe."

"Crewe?! You're kidding? You're not a wind-sock salesman, by any chance?" Ray laughed out loud at his own joke. No-one else did.

"No, that wasn't me. But I've heard about him."

Elizabeth couldn't stand it any longer. She had foolishly let her guard down, but now it was back with a vengeance. "You're in on this together, aren't you? You've set this whole thing up." She got to her feet, kicking Barney's rucksack towards him under the table. He gave a little yelp and rubbed his shin. "Who the hell are you?" she cried. "I don't carry any cash with me, you know."

Barney was still rubbing his sore shin. "Cash? What does she mean?" he said, a little nonplussed.

"I've had enough of this." Elizabeth picked up her bag and shuffled sideways towards the aisle of the carriage. She was just about to start moving towards the door when Ray put out a hand to stop her.

"You really did think you were the only one, didn't you?"

Elizabeth tried as hard as she could to ignore the question. She took a step towards the door. This time Barney stopped her.

"You can't get off. This is only your first stop." The young man looked genuinely disturbed at the woman's flagrant disregard for the rules.

Before Elizabeth had a chance to say, 'Just you watch me,' a whistle blew and the train lurched into action again.

120

She lost her balance for a moment and grabbed hold of the headrest on the empty seat beside her. She didn't know what to do next. Maybe she should carry on and walk straight to the next carriage. Maybe she should scream for help. Maybe she should just sit back down and concede defeat. She did none of those things. Instead, she just stood there, awkward and out of place. Not wanting to be where she was, but being too frightened of being anywhere else in case it was worse. This was her whole seventh train journey in microcosm.

The two men continued their conversation as if Elizabeth had simply chosen to stand there for some mysterious 'woman's' reason. "How many others have you met, Barney?" asked Ray breezily.

"You two are the fifth and sixth, but I've never met two Seventh Trainers travelling together before."

Elizabeth shoved her shopping bag back down on the empty seat opposite Barney and turned to the men, planting her feet firmly on the floor to stop her body from swaying wildly with the train. "We are *not* travelling together. Whatever he says."

Without giving Elizabeth the satisfaction of a direct response, and to add to her growing frustration, Ray leaned in towards Barney and said confidentially: "I think we are now, don't you?"

"I think it's nice," said Barney. "It makes the whole thing more interesting, doesn't it?"

"I couldn't agree more, my friend." Ray glanced up at Elizabeth, gave her a friendly wink and motioned for her to sit back down.

Welcome aboard this Greater Anglia rail service to Ipswich, calling at Newmarket, Kennett, Bury St Edmunds, Stowmarket and Ipswich. Thank you for travelling with us today.

Elizabeth manoeuvred herself roughly past the aisle seat and sat back down heavily in the window seat opposite Ray. The two men watched while she re-arranged her shopping bag; checking that all its contents were still there after knocking it sideways in her impatience to look casual. "I can always get off at the next stop, if I want to."

"Of course you can," appeased Ray.

"But you shouldn't," added Barney with a frown. His furrowed brow made him look even younger and a little helpless; like a child who asks simple questions that adults can't answer. Ray put out his hand to pat the lad on the arm, as if to say, 'it's OK. Sometimes adults just don't know.'

"What I should and shouldn't do," Elizabeth retorted, "is really none of your concern." And she lifted the strap of her handbag off her shoulder and put it down on the table between her and the two men. It was a deliberate act of defiance. She wished, at that moment, that she was clever with words. If only she could pull out some other witty retort to imply that she was not only sharp, but dangerous too. She had nothing.

The train rumbled on. The ticket inspector breezed into the carriage again, saw that there were no new tickets to collect, and breezed out again, whistling as he went. The few streets and houses that made up the village of Dullingham – a place that none of them had heard of before and that all of them would forget, if they were asked in the future where they'd been – had given way to flat fields and the occasional horse. The rain had eased and the sky had lightened to became a pale blanket of grey. Everything outside the windows of the carriage looked calm and peaceful and normal.

Ray leaned back in his seat and placed his hands casually behind his head again, only just missing Barney's face in the process. He was settling himself into the journey and deriving a great deal of pleasure from having travelling companions to share it with. It was good to have an audience again. He gazed back at Elizabeth through half-closed eyes. He could see she wasn't enjoying the adventure half as much as he was. There were tell-tale signs in the way she was holding the tension around her mouth and eyes. Even her hair looked clenched. "You should learn to relax a bit more," he suggested.

Elizabeth threw him her best attempt at a withering glance. "Should I, now?"

"Yes, you should," nodded Ray. "Have you ever thought of taking up meditation?"

It was difficult to tell whether this was a genuine piece of advice or just subtle sarcasm. Elizabeth opened her mouth, in the hope that, by some miracle, a witty riposte was now waiting. There wasn't one. She closed her mouth again, folded her arms and tutted instead.

"It would do you good." It *had* been genuine advice, albeit misguided. But then Ray had never been known for his sensitivity when speaking to women – Mabel Heep could attest to that. So could Maroon. In fact, he wasn't always that sensitive with men either. He spoke to everyone as if he were either addressing a room full of first-year students or talking to himself in a mirror. The first was always just teetering on the edge of condescension, and the second was just shy of ego-mania. "Arnold Schwarzenegger once taught me this incredibly effective breathing technique, if you're interested."

This last, almost throwaway name-drop, piqued Barney's interest and he became instantly animated. He twisted himself round in his chair and seized Ray's leg. "You know Arnie? Wow! That is so cool!"

Ray retrieved his hands from behind his head and, with lazy, self-assured grace, removed Barney's excited hand from his thigh, put it flat on the table and patted it gently. "Yes," he said. "You wouldn't think it to look at him, but Arnie's fanatical about Hatha Yoga. I can take you through it when we get off the train, if you like." Elizabeth simply tutted again.

"Cool," repeated Barney. He took his hand back from the table, put it in his lap with the other one and began to twiddle his fingers. He looked down at them and spoke a little sadly. "That was your first stop, wasn't it?"

Ray nodded. "Yep. Looks like we're going to Bury St Edmunds today."

Elizabeth wanted to interject and disagree. She was going nowhere with these people, but she felt she'd said enough. Fearing her 'tuts' were in danger of becoming repetitive, and not wanting to come across as some bitter, middle-aged woman, she chose to shrug her shoulders and give a little 'huff' instead.

"That was my second stop," said Barney, still focusing on his twiddling fingers. I got on before you." His disappointment was palpable. He hadn't yet told

124

his story, and now he looked like a little boy who'd just had his birthday party cancelled. Ray punched the young man playfully on the arm in a fraternal gesture of encouragement. The action looked unnatural coming from him; like dogs dressed as humans, or priests strumming *Motorhead* songs on acoustic guitars. Barney stopped twiddling his fingers and rubbed his arm. Ray apologised immediately. He didn't know his own strength.

"We still have some time before you get off," said Ray, trying to make amends for the small bruise that was already darkening under Barney's overalls. "Come on, lad. What's *your* story?"

"Oh, great," snorted Elizabeth. "Another story to pass the time."

Barney spoke kindly in response. This woman was clearly new to all this. "We all tell our stories when we meet another Seventh Trainer," he explained. "It's become a sort of unspoken rule. Nobody knows who started it, but that's just what we do."

It occurred to Elizabeth that she'd done precisely that, back in Cambridge, sitting in the station café with Ellie. She felt a little shiver run down her spine but kept her composure. "I'm sorry. I didn't realise there were rules. Do forgive me gentlemen," she said with mock deference.

"You have to have rules," justified Barney, "otherwise the seventh train would all be random – and it's not."

Ray took up the argument. "Otherwise why would you be counting trains like this, dear lady?"

Elizabeth couldn't explain why. She decided to change tack instead. "How do you know if the story is true? Answer me that."

"We don't," replied Ray and Barney in unison. The men looked at each other, smiled and attempted another unwise high-five. Ray missed and hit the seat, both men ignored the error and looked at Elizabeth for the next move. Luckily for her, the woman with the perfect voice interjected. Her timing was impeccable.

Welcome aboard this Greater Anglia rail service to Ipswich. For your safety and convenience, customers are advised to familiarise themselves with the safety procedures displayed inside the carriage. Thank you for travelling with us today.

Barney's eyes lit up at this latest announcement. "Have you both read the safety instructions, by the way?" Ray and Elizabeth looked at each other blankly and then at Barney. Did anyone ever read them?

"I think we'll be fine," said Ray with unnecessary condescension.

Barney shook his head in disgust and sat up straight to make his point straighter. "You *should* read them, you know. It's important to know the difference between a button and a handle."

Ray resisted a mocking smile. He was growing fond of his new young friend and didn't want to hurt his feelings. An unusual state of affairs for him. "I'd rather hear your story first, Barney."

"*Then* you'll read them?"

"Yes, of course we will," Ray looked for back up, "won't we… er, I still don't know your name."

Elizabeth wasn't about to give up her identity so easily.

She needed to keep some of herself back. She sidestepped the question and replied to Barney instead. "If it makes you feel better, we'll read the safety instructions."

"Yes, it does." Barney became more animated as he explained. "Because I've noticed that most people on trains never bother to read them at all." That was undoubtedly true. "It's like planes, isn't it?" He paused for consensus, but all that came back were blank, slightly patronising looks. "It's true. The cabin crew get really annoyed when people don't watch them going through the safety procedures, you know." Still there were only blank looks in return; patient and polite though they were. "For example, do you know where the exits are in this carriage?"

"Yes," interjected Elizabeth. "Right through *that* door, where I'm going as soon as this train stops again."

"Well, that's where you're wrong." Barney got up from his seat, stepped into the aisle of the carriage and proceeded to illustrate in his best air steward imitation, pointing his hands towards all eight of the emergency exits that were clearly marked above doors and windows. There were more of them than Elizabeth and Ray had realised. They were just like everybody else. They hadn't even picked up the safety procedures that had been printed, laminated, and left in little receptacles throughout the carriage.

"Well, I never," remarked Ray. "I am impressed." And he gave Barney a short round of applause in recognition of this young man actually teaching him something that he didn't already know.

Barney took the applause with a little raise of his chin and a stiffening of his posture. "And people think they know what to do in the event of an emergency, but they really don't. More people get injured because of that." He sat down, satisfied. "That might save your life one day."

All these journeys and all these stops; getting off and counting trains and getting on again. It had never occurred to Elizabeth to read instructions or check for emergency exits. She'd really only thought about keeping safe by staying alone and isolated from any other travellers. When she had to interact, she preferred to lie and invent; to indulge herself like she had tried to do back at Cambridge station. Now she looked at Barney sitting opposite her. There was an obvious childlike quality to him, which was evident to anyone. He reminded her of Ellie. It was something about the way he held himself, or the lack of guile in his eyes and in his words. But he wasn't as simple as he looked either. Watching the care and urgency in his short safety demonstration spoke of a greater depth. Ray was right. Everybody has a story to tell. And, as her mother used to say when she was a little girl: 'You never know who you're sitting next to.' "Thanks Barney," she said. And she meant it.

"Right then," Ray clapped his hands then rubbed them together in anticipation. "Are you going to regale us with your story before we get to the next station, Barney? We're running out of time."

Barney frowned and dug his heels in. "Only if you promise to read the safety instructions afterwards."

"We promise," said Ray.

"I need to hear you say it too."

"Yes," said Elizabeth. "I promise."

Chapter Eight:
The First Train from Crewe

I love parks… No, that's not quite right. I love parks, but I really love the grassy bits the best. Always have. Not just in parks either – football pitches, garden lawns, tennis courts, anywhere that has neat, green grass.

When I was a little boy, my social worker reckoned it was because neatly cut grass represents order, and that was something that had been missing from my childhood. I grew up in care, you see, and there wasn't much order in there; just rules, and that's not the same thing. My social worker was called Abi. She was nice. I liked her, but I think she talked too much. She used to get all nervous and twitchy at the end of our sessions. This is because she smoked but pretended that she didn't. You could smell it on her clothes. When she got nervous she used to put her pen between her fingers and roll it around like it was a cigarette. I used to watch to see if she would forget one day, put the pen in her mouth and light it with a match. It would have been funny if she did. She didn't, though. She was a professional.

It wasn't my mum's fault that I went into care. She couldn't cope, so they took me away when I was five years old. A man and a lady came with a big, grey car and put me inside it. They didn't tell me what was happening, they just spoke really slowly all the time as if I couldn't understand them. It was the depression. That's what I was told when I was a bit older. It made it hard for my mum to do the things that mums are supposed to do. I've never had depression. I've been sad lots of times, like everybody, I guess, but I've always been able to carry on and do what I'm supposed to do. Some boys in the care home didn't know how to handle being sad, and they got into trouble for it. Maybe they had depression too. I don't know. Perhaps some of them did. Some of them were probably just angry.

It might have been my dad's fault, but I don't know because I never knew him. I don't think I ever asked them at the home about my dad, and I don't remember anyone ever talking to me about him. I've never even seen a photograph. I'd like to one day, just in case I look like him. If I do, and if I knew what he looked like now, I'd be able to see what I will look like when I'm old. That would be interesting.

I used to ask the people in the home how my mum was doing. They would always say, "She's fine but she's not very well." I got two letters from her and I kept them both for a long time in the bottom of my sock drawer. I only read them once each. That was enough because they did make me sad. After that, I just used to take them out and look at the envelopes, tracing the spidery handwriting on the front with my finger. I wanted to write my words the same way so that I could say, 'I get that from my mum,' because I'm not sure if I've got anything else from her. The thing is, I'm not always very good at concentrating when I write things down. My words always come out sort of round and leaning to the left. So, I definitely didn't get handwriting or depression from my mum. I'm not even sure if I look like her because I've forgotten her face. She had long, red hair, that's all I remember. I don't know what happened to the letters. Somebody probably found them and ripped them up for a joke. That sort of thing used to happen a lot.

Some of the boys in the care home were fostered out from time to time, or even adopted. Some of them were collected again by parents who came and cried and took them away, holding their hands tight when they left. That didn't happen to me. I think it's because I was very quiet most of the time and not all that good at school. I was a bit chubby for my age too, and foster parents don't seem to like that. Maybe they think you'll be too expensive to feed.

I did love biology, though, because it was all about nature. That's the only thing I was good at when I was at school. Everything else was just too hard to get right. There was this big garden round the back of the home that backed onto playing fields where we did rugby and football with Mr Cooper. I used to sit in the garden a lot just studying the trees and the birds and looking at the grass. I used to take paper and pencils with me to try and draw all the different things that I saw. I'm not brilliant at drawing, but the pictures were really useful. When you're trying to think, or understand something, you have to have something to do with your hands, otherwise people assume you're doing nothing and they tell you off for daydreaming or tease you like you're stupid. If you're doing something with your hands, they think you're being creative and useful so they leave you alone. It's funny, but it's true. You can't see 'thinking,' but you can see 'doing.' Anyway, I sat in that garden for hours and hours with my paper and pencils. I watched and I learnt what time of year the grass grew the quickest and when it needed cutting and when it needed to be left alone, and how many different types of grass there are. There's a lot to learn, if you know how to watch. And if you have a bit of patience.

When I was old enough to take care of myself – legally, I mean – Abi did everything she could to help me get a job so that I could leave the care home and start paying for myself. She spent almost a whole afternoon asking what I liked, telling me what I was good at, and filling out lots of different forms. I didn't get a job straight away. I didn't even get an interview for a while, just a few letters that all wished me luck. They didn't have to do that. I remember that I used to pray back then, every night before I went to bed. It's not because I believed in God, I still haven't made up my mind about that because it's a lot to think about. I prayed because Mrs Denton at the care home used to tell us to do it, and she was one of the kind ones. Not everyone there was like her. I grew up to think that whatever you wanted you could get it if you really, really believed when you prayed for it, just because Mrs Denton said so and I trusted her. I can't tell you if that's actually true, but it worked for me. I couldn't have asked for a more perfect job than the one I eventually got. It was the very first job interview I ever had, and the last. I haven't said any prayers since. I'd asked for other things before and never got them. I thought, maybe it's like winning the lottery or meeting your soul mate. You only get those things once in your life, if you're lucky, so there's no point trying again. You'll only be disappointed. I do know that there are people who *have* won the lottery more than once, but that's very, very rare. There's more chance of being abducted by aliens – and that's a fact.

Anyway, my prayer was answered and I became an assistant park keeper, employed by the local council. I would get to be in the park every day and get paid for it. It was absolutely brilliant. I got proper park keeper overalls, wellies, and everything, and I got them all for free, as long as I looked after them – and I did. I felt like a man for the first time. And, with all that fresh air and exercise, I dropped all the chubbiness and started to feel fit and strong. I wouldn't have looked so expensive to feed anymore if any of those foster parents could have seen me. Mind you, I was eating more than ever. It must have been all the fresh air. I always remembered to have breakfast, made myself sandwiches for lunch, and was still hungry by three o'clock every day.

At first everything was amazing; even better than I could have imagined. My boss, the head keeper, was called Phil, and he was a really sound bloke. He taught me all the proper names of the trees and the flowers and told me which birds made what sounds, that kind of thing. Once I showed him the pictures I'd drawn in the care home garden. He said, "That's nice, boy," and asked if he could keep one. He really took me under his wing; looked after me, you know. He became like a second father. Actually, come to think of it, he was more like a first one because mine didn't really count. Phil asked me one day: "Do you miss your father, lad?" I just shrugged my shoulders and told him that my social worker once said, 'you don't miss what you've never had.' Phil never asked me about him again. I think it's because he agreed with what Abi said. I was glad, because I agreed with it too.

After six months of training, Phil put me in charge of the big lawns near the entrance gates to the park. They're beautiful. Big and flat and smooth. There are five round beds in the middle of the lawns, full of all kinds of flowers that change during the year so that there's always colour for people to see. I wasn't allowed to be in charge of the flowers, though. Phil carried on looking after those, but he did let me help him with the weeding and the digging and keeping them tidy. He said I could design my own flower beds one day, but first I had to prove that I could look after the grass. He said it was very important to learn how to do it well because a picture is nothing without the right frame.

Phil didn't need to try and convince me. I reckon he thought that the grass wasn't really as important as the flowers, but the lawns were already my favourite. It was my job to keep them watered and fed and raked, and to mow them so that all the grass was always just the right length. Through the middle was a neat little path that went from one side to the other, and around the flowerbeds so that people could walk to them and smell the blooms, without treading on my grass. I had a special pair of lawn scissors so that I could trim the grass around the edges of the path, and I always tried to make it look perfect. I don't know whether anyone ever noticed or not. I didn't mind either way. Phil noticed, and it made him happy. It made both of us happy, although sometimes he complained that I took too long with the lawn scissors. "That will do, lad," he used to say. "There's no such thing as perfect. That grass will start growing again as soon as you look away." I worked at the park for almost five years. Phil never did put me in charge of the flowerbeds.

I can still picture every inch of that park in my mind. We had little wooden signs everywhere that said 'Keep Off the Grass,' and we really meant it. That grass was as close to perfect as you can get and it needed to be kept safe. That was the rules. We had other rules too: 'No Cycling,' 'Dogs Must Be Kept On Leads At All Times,' 'No Nudity In The Hedges,' that kind of thing. And I thought that was right. I loved the rules at first. I guess I needed order, just like Abi said.

Then one morning – I remember it was a Thursday morning to be exact – I was raking up some leaves under the big beech trees near the gate and making them into a pile, like I do. I was trying to make the pile as neat as possible and stop the leaves from blowing about in the breeze. It was taking up all my concentration, so I didn't see the little boy who came haring through the gate and into the park. He was no more than three or four years old, and he was running about on *my* grass without a care in the world; stamping his little red wellies all over it. He wasn't just running and stamping either; he was rolling himself around on it, laughing and screaming his head off like crazy, and as he rolled, his little hands grabbed big clumps of grass and he pulled them out and threw them above his head so that they fell on him like green snow. I dropped my rake and ran across to where he was still rolling around. I shouted at him, I said: "Oi! You! Keep off the grass! Can't you read the sign?" Of course, he couldn't read it, could he? He was only a little kid. I realise that now. He probably didn't even see the sign.

Then his mum ran over all frantic from God knows where, calling out: "Freddie! Freddie! Come here now!" I hadn't seen her at first. I was too busy shouting at her little Freddie to get off my grass. She was breathing hard and all red in the face, like she wasn't used to running at all; not like her little boy. She wasn't angry at me, though. I thought she would be, but I suppose she could see I was just trying to do my job. And I never actually touched the boy. I wouldn't. I know what it's like to be slapped by someone bigger than you, and you don't forget it. Anyway, his mum stomped across the grass with big, square heels on her boots before I could stop her. I was the only one who should be walking on that grass. I could have got him off there without doing any more damage. The boy was still rolling and pulling out the grass when his mum got to him. She grabbed him by the arm, lifted him onto his feet with one hand, and pulled him off the grass, really rough, like. She kept saying sorry to me, all embarrassed, and shouting at him not to run off again while she stomped across the lawn and onto the path with her clumpy boots. I didn't say anything. But I really, really wanted to.

It was the boy that stopped me saying anything else. He cried his little eyes out, didn't he? Big, fat tears were streaming down his face and he sobbed so loud that all the pigeons in the beech trees flew away. He looked back at me as his mum dragged him out of the park, wagging her finger at him and trying to quieten him down. I'll never forget the look on that little boy's face. He was devastated. It was like... like his whole little world had changed forever. He had complete and total disappointment all over his face. Yes. That's what it was. He looked like he was disappointed at all of us grown-ups; disappointed about his whole future as one of us, including me. I was devastated too. I broke a little boy's heart that day. He was only playing, wasn't he?

And that's when it happened. I realised that I'd forgotten what it was like to be an innocent little boy. I don't remember when it stopped; the total joy of rolling about on the grass, just like I used to do in the big garden at the care home when nobody was watching; loving the freedom of throwing myself around the soft, green grass and feeling it all over my face. For five years in the park, I'd been trying so hard to make the lawns perfect that I'd forgotten why I loved them. It wasn't the little boy's fault, it was mine. I think I stole his childhood single-handedly that day. I could hear him crying all the way out of the park. I looked at that lawn. I knew every blade of grass on it. I'd looked after it lovingly for all that time like it was my own baby. I watered it, fed it, protected it from harm. But, now, it didn't look so perfect any more. It wasn't because of the loose bits that the boy had pulled out as he rolled about. It wasn't even the holes that his mother's boots had made when she stomped across it. It was my fault. I'd forgotten why I loved the grass. After work, I went straight home and I thought about my mum for the first time in years.

The next morning, I got up really, really early and got to the park way before Phil and me were due to start work. He was always ten minutes late anyway. I don't know why, but it was always ten minutes exactly. I never asked him about it because he was the boss. I went to the big shed, undid the padlock, and got my spade and a wheelbarrow out of it. Then I went to the piece of grass where the little boy had been rolling – I knew exactly which bit it was – and I dug up a perfect square patch of it, all in one big chunk, with my spade. I carefully picked it up and put the

137

fresh turf in the wheelbarrow, then I took it to the bench near the children's playground and waited.

Just before nine o'clock, the little boy turned up with his mum to play on the swings – him, not his mum. She was just there to push him, although I reckon they should have swings and roundabouts for grown-ups in the park too. I'd thought a lot about exactly what I was going to do, and I did it just like I planned. I wheeled the square bit of turf over to the little boy, took it out of the wheelbarrow and held it out to him in both my hands. The damp, dark soil under the grass felt cold between my fingers. I held it out and I said to him, "Here you go, lad. You can play on *this* grass whenever you like. It's yours."

The little boy smiled. He just smiled. His mum stared at me with her mouth wide open and then pulled the boy away. I thought she might at least say, 'thank you,' but she didn't. She didn't say anything to me; not to my face. Instead she started muttering to herself out loud that I must be some kind of nutter or something. But for her son it was different. That little boy smiled a huge, wide grin at me. A big, fat grin, right back at me, and then he laughed and clapped his hands. His mum grabbed one of those hands in hers so that he couldn't clap anymore, but he was still grinning. I watched them both walk out of the park until they were well out of sight. Every now and again his mum would look back in my direction and frown while she was dragging him off, as if to say: 'You better not come near my boy again.' But I didn't want to. I'd done what I came to do, and that was it.

The square bit of damp turf was still in my hands. Nobody else was in the children's playground, and I don't think anybody had been there the whole time. I wouldn't have cared if they were. This was about the little boy and me and nobody else. I carried the piece of grass to the swings and put it down carefully on the ground next to the one that his mother had pushed him on. That way the little boy could find it again the next time he came to the park. The playground is covered with that black, rubber matting that they put down for safety, in case some kid falls down and cracks his head. The grass looked odd sitting on it, but it also looked perfect. I put my spade in the wheelbarrow, took them both back to the big shed, locked it all up, and walked out of the park.

I went home to tidy my little bedsit, do the washing up and make some sandwiches. I brushed my teeth, put some clean clothes, a towel, my wash bag, and the sandwiches in my rucksack, and left a note for the landlord to say that he could have anything that I'd left behind to pay for whatever I owed in rent. There wasn't very much to leave. Just the bedclothes, a few dirty socks and some gardening magazines. Maybe a couple of other bits and pieces. The rest of the stuff was his anyway. Then I walked to Crewe station and got on the seventh train that came into the station. I'm not sure why I decided to get on the seventh and not the third or the ninth. It just seemed right at the time. I had no idea where I was going, I just knew I had to go somewhere else. I had to take myself away before I could do any more damage.

When I think about it, I really wish I'd said goodbye to Phil. It makes me sad that I didn't. He was always good to me. I sent him a postcard from Blackpool a couple of weeks after I left. It had a picture of a donkey wearing a hat covered in flowers on the front. I'd never been to the seaside before. I tried to explain why I had left without saying anything. I wrote to him that I had to try and remember something I'd forgotten. I wonder if he understood. I don't know. And I wonder if that little boy ever found the grass that I put next to the swings. I hope so – to both of those things.

Chapter Nine:
Newmarket Station

"There you are!" A familiar, excitable voice burst into the train carriage like a summer thunderstorm. The three passengers at the table sat up as one and craned their necks towards the door like a family of meerkats.

"Ellie!" cried Elizabeth. "What the hell are you doing here?"

It was perfect timing. Barney had just finished as much as he wanted to share of his story. His mouth hung open as he watched a young woman in red and black shoes struggling down the aisle with an overstuffed, brightly-coloured, heavy-looking suitcase. "Wow!" he said. "It must be a convention! This has never happened before." Ray just smiled smugly, as if he'd expected the girl to turn up all along.

Ellie manhandled her suitcase the last few feet until she was level with the table where the other three sat still, Barney still gawping in amazement. She caught her breath then tried to catch her balance, swaying with the train and bumping herself between the seats like a doll in a pinball machine. She put out her hand to grab Elizabeth's arm across the empty aisle seat, missed, and ended up half sprawled across the table. She smiled up at Elizabeth, as if she'd meant to land exactly there. "Hiya!" she chirped in greeting. "I got on your seventh train but I couldn't find you. I've been sat in the flippin' Quiet Carriage." Ellie straightened herself up and pulled back a thick strand of hair that had fallen over her face. It fell back down and she blew at it noisily a couple of times before forcing it roughly behind her ear.

The whole thing looked deliciously droll to everyone except Elizabeth. "What happened?" she asked. Elizabeth was serious, and it showed in her face.

"I was asked to leave," said Ellie rolling her eyes in disgust. "Another passenger complained. They said I was too noisy, apparently." She sucked her teeth in disgust.

Ray let out a loud guffaw. Barney still looked bemused. Elizabeth glared at them both. She was concerned for the young woman. Unlike Ray, she hadn't expected this turn of events at all. "No, I mean why aren't you on your way to Brighton like you're supposed to be?"

Ellie opened out her arms like she deserved a big hug. "Because the world is my flippin' lobster, that's why!" The train lurched around a bend and Ellie sprawled back across the table. Ray put out his hands to catch her and Ellie could now look him straight in the eye. She recognised the man immediately and with eagerness. "Oh, hello!" she cried, "it's the weirdo from the café – no offence."

"None taken." Ray stood up and helped Ellie back to a standing position with some difficulty and with assistance from Barney. Once she was steady again, he made his formal introduction. "My name is Ray, but you can call me 'weirdo' if you prefer."

"Nah. I'll call you Ray… Alright, Ray?" She was too adorable to reproach, like a new puppy that's just pooped in your best saucepan. Ray tilted his head and smiled. He almost said 'Awww,' but stopped himself in time. The girl might feel that was patronising.

Ellie pulled her suitcase the last few inches down the aisle until it stood squarely in front of her and then attempted, in vain, to lift it off the floor and onto the overhead luggage rack. It was evident that she couldn't possibly heft it more than a couple of inches. Barney got to his feet with a polite, 'allow me,' then lifted the suitcase easily into position. It hung over the edge of the rack precariously, its multi-coloured hearts beaming out at the carriage like over-friendly danger signs. Barney reached back up and slid the suitcase, with some difficulty, along and past their table until it hung over the one behind, just in case it should fall and crush one of his companions.

"You're a big, strong boy," said Ellie, impressed. Barney blushed and sat back down. "Right, shove up then." Elizabeth moved her shopping bag off the seat next to her and placed it carefully under the table between her feet. She clamped it with her ankles to make sure she'd be able to feel that it was there the whole time. Ellie sat down heavily in the vacant aisle seat, took a deep breath and relaxed herself into this newest part of her adventure. "And... breathe," she said, letting out a long, loud sigh. She stuffed her big, pink shoulder bag between herself and the arm rest, where it bulged out into the aisle, shook out her hands, smoothed down her hair, and was ready to proceed. "So, where are we all going, then?"

"Bury St Edmunds," said Ray.

Elizabeth felt a wave of panic hit her in the stomach. This was turning out all wrong. She wished the café hadn't been so full at Cambridge station. She wished now that she'd lied and said that she was saving the spare seat for someone. She wished that she'd been more cautious and said nothing to this girl about what she was doing or why. She wished that she really was a hotel inspector. "Oh, Ellie, my dear girl, I told you that was all nonsense. I was just making it up."

Ellie brushed off the comment. "Yeah, I know. I'm so gullible." She really wasn't that stupid, but she found that it often paid to pretend she was. She turned her attention away from Elizabeth's worried face to the big, strong boy in the seat opposite. "Hello. What's your name then?"

"I'm Barney."

"Hi Barney, I'm Ellie." She thrust out her hand with a happy, wide smile. Barney shook it and smiled back with far less confidence. If he was chalk, this young woman was definitely cheese. Not just mild English Cheddar either; more like some strong, exotic French cheese that comes in fancy cardboard boxes, that's how different they were. "I'm Ellie. Pleased to meet you, Barney." She motioned with her thumb towards Elizabeth like they were in cahoots. "We're doing the seventh train," she exclaimed proudly.

"Me too," said Barney.

"Shut – up! Really?" cried Ellie, sitting up equally straight. She turned to Elizabeth. "You never said there were others."

"I didn't know," said Elizabeth. "I'm just as surprised as you are." She turned in her seat to face the girl squarely, trying desperately to think of other ways to put her off joining them. She didn't have a chance because Barney got in first.

"Your friends here are going to Bury St Edmunds."

"Cool," said Ellie. She paused and eyed her companions one by one. Ray had settled back with his hands behind his head again, surveying the funny little party around the table with a satisfied grin on his face. Elizabeth looked a little agitated, but Ellie put that down to excitement at discovering she hadn't gone to Brighton after all but chosen to travel with her new pal. Barney just looked confused but happy. "Where's Bury St Edmunds?" said Ellie.

"I have no idea," said Barney.

"So, where are *you* going then?"

Barney's face fell. He looked down at the table, his expression growing gloomy. "I'm getting off the stop before," he said quietly.

Ellie reached out her hand but stopped just short of touching Barney. She tapped her fingers on the table in front of him instead in the hope that he might look up at her. He didn't. She took her hand back and softened her voice. "Why aren't you travelling with us?"

"Yes, Barney," echoed Ray. "Why aren't you travelling with us?"

It was a clumsy attempt at evasion, but Barney managed to sidestep the question by focusing on his effervescent new companion. "I've been telling your friends here my story about how I started doing the seventh train."

"That's awesome," said Ellie.

"Yeah, we all do it," explained Barney. "I'll tell you about it some other time, if you like. Maybe. If we bump into each other somewhere on the trains."

Ray leaned across to interject with the intention of filling out some of the story for Ellie so that she could catch up. Once a storyteller, always a storyteller. "Barney was explaining how it all started with his love of grass."

Ellie nodded her head with a knowing kind of smile. "Oh, right," she said. "I had some grass once."

Was this the soul mate that Barney had always hoped to meet one day? He wondered if it could be true. Suddenly, unexpectedly, the girl sitting opposite looked more beautiful, more captivating than he ever remembered any woman looking before. "Really?" he cooed.

"Yeah," replied Ellie, entirely unconscious of the interest she had stirred in Barney's deepest recesses. "Me and my mate Chelsea were watching *Deal or No Deal* on TV, and she laughed so hard at box twenty-two that she threw up all over the *LazeeBoy*." She paused for a big, expressive shrug of her shoulders. "I still don't know what was so funny. I just ate three *Mars* bars and got a headache."

Elizabeth covered her eyes and sighed. Ray enjoyed Ellie's revelation rather more and let out a loud snort of amusement. Barney just looked ever so slightly confused and sunk back into his seat. Maybe this wasn't his soul mate after all.

"I don't think Barney meant that kind of grass, Ellie," said Elizabeth.

"Didn't he?"

"No, I didn't," confirmed Barney, and a tiny piece of his romantic hopes and dreams died forever.

We will shortly be arriving at Newmarket; Newmarket is your next station stop. Please remember to collect all of your personal belongings when leaving the train.

"Two," said Ray.

"Two," said Elizabeth.

"Two – yay!" cried Ellie.

"Three. Dammit!" cursed Barney.

"Which brings me back to our previous question." Ray suddenly remembered that it was as yet unanswered. "Why aren't you travelling with us, Barney?"

"I *am* travelling with you."

"No," insisted Ray, "I mean beyond the next stop; beyond the next train?"

"Seriously," added Ellie, "aren't you getting off with us? It might be a laugh." And she flashed a big smile at Barney as if it was a taster of all the laughs yet to come. He wasn't convinced.

"No, I can't," resisted Barney. "I got on this train one stop earlier than all of you, so I'm one stop ahead."

Ellie was not one to be put off so easily; not when there was some promise of adventure and new people to play with. "That's okay," she assured Barney, in a manner so breezy that he could almost feel it on his face. "You can just do five stops instead of four."

"Five?!" Barney called the word out as if he were in pain. "I can't do that!" He was absolutely horrified at the suggestion that he should break the rules, and for somebody that he'd only known for five minutes, no matter how attractive he thought she was.

The debate between Ellie and Barney continued for a few more rounds. Unreasonable arguments and lame excuses were lobbed backwards and forwards in a futile game that went around and around getting absolutely nowhere. By this time, Ray had retrieved his black notebook from his pocket and was scribbling furiously, enjoying the little game of persuasion and refusal immensely, but Elizabeth had had enough. She reached down between her ankles, grabbed her bag and pulled it up roughly until it was sitting on her lap. Then she retrieved her handbag from the table, where it had been sat all this time between her and Ray, and replaced the strap over her head and across her body where it usually belonged. "That's it," she exclaimed, banging the table. She hadn't intended on being so melodramatic, and the loud rattle of the table surprised her as much as it did everyone else. It had the desired effect, however, and the other three stopped, frozen in mid action, and looked at Elizabeth. She seized the opportunity to assert herself as best she could – something she really wasn't used to. It felt good at the time. "Right! I've had enough. Let me out, Ellie." She got to her feet and started to move towards the aisle of the carriage. She didn't get very far.

Ellie refused to comply and stayed sitting rigidly in her seat. "Where are you going?" she asked.

"You can't get off," added Barney, "We're moving."

Right on cue, the train lurched around a bend and Elizabeth was thrown unceremoniously back down on to her seat with a thud. She exhaled a loud breath of weary frustration. "I'm not getting off, I'm moving to another carriage," she said. "I've had enough of all this."

"Now, now, love," said Ray. He meant to use the words in a calming way in an effort to persuade Elizabeth to stay and relax. Unfortunately for him, they just came out as condescending and a little bit sexist. That wasn't a good idea.

Elizabeth snapped and rounded on Ray. "First of all, I'm not your love." Then, turning to Ellie by way of a plea from one who's older to one who's younger and doesn't know any better: "And as for you – as sweet a girl as you are, I never asked anyone to come with me on this journey; not you, and certainly not them."

There was a loud intake of breath from Ray. "That was a bit harsh."

His comment was ignored without effort. "And anyway, my dear, you have no idea who these two men are. They could be up to anything. Didn't your parents teach you not to talk to strange men?"

"Hey!" said Barney. "What does she mean by that?" Ray patted him on the arm and shook his head, assuring him that it was nothing to worry about. It was probably just a little female over-anxiety. Happens all the time. Surprisingly, Barney understood what Ray meant completely from his body language, but still felt a little bit offended.

"Safety in numbers, ain't it?" shrugged Ellie. "Anyway, they flippin' try anything and we push the emergency button – simple as."

"It's a handle on these trains," corrected Barney. "It's not a button. And definitely not a cord."

"He's right," said Ray.

"Whatever." Ellie didn't really care whether it was a button, a handle or a mushroom risotto. She continued trying to convince Elizabeth, despite her protestations. "Mind you," said Ellie, "I could probably beat the older one up if I really had to." She looked Ray up and down by way of confirming the matter to herself, realised that he had clearly been taken aback by what she said and then reached out a hand to him. "No offence," she said.

"A little bit taken," said Ray. He took her hand anyway and shook it as firmly as he could. A handshake is always a test of strength between males, so he was used to having to prove what he was made of. Unfortunately for Ray, Ellie's grip was quite a bit stronger than his. He let her hand go, flexed his fingers a couple of times, then scribbled a few sentences in his notebook. Barney leaned over in an attempt to sneak a peek at what was so interesting that it had to be documented, but Ray covered the page with his other arm as he continued to scribble. Barney took the hint and sat back.

Ellie continued, ignoring the scribbling altogether. "I'm just along for the ride," she explained to the group, although nobody had asked her to clarify. "If I get bored I can just get off the train and go back home. Or," she added, "I could go to Brighton, if I want. There's still time."

"No, you can't!" Barney was horrified at this suggestion. "That's not in the rules. Tell her, Ray."

But Ray was too busy finishing off his last sentence. He put down his pen and had a quick scan at what he'd written, nodded to himself with satisfaction, and put his notebook back in the inside pocket of his jacket. He looked round at his companions. Barney was still staring at him with anticipation of some kind of endorsement. "What?" asked Ray blankly. "Did you say something, Barney?"

"Tell her," repeated Barney, pointing at Ellie with a nervous finger. "Tell her it's not in the rules."

"What rules?" asked Ellie.

Barney's voice had gone up an octave in pitch and started wobbling slightly. It made him sound like a little boy protesting his innocence when wrongly accused of breaking a window. "She said she can get off this train whenever she likes."

"So?" shrugged Ray. "She can. We all can. Or you can carry on travelling forever. It's up to you."

That was enough to cause Barney to break out in a sweat. He undid the top button on his overalls and rubbed his hot neck with an even hotter hand. "This has been a really strange train," he said.

Elizabeth and Ray could both see how uncomfortable the young man was becoming. Perhaps it was their age, or perhaps it was Barney's natural naivety, but his senior companions both felt an overwhelming urge to soothe him. They looked at each other in a knowing kind of way. Elizabeth motioned to Ray to say something. A distraction technique might work best, he thought, as it does with parents trying to stop children from discovering something they shouldn't. "I tell you what, Barney," suggested Ray, "why don't you show Ellie the safety instructions at the back there." He motioned towards the framed notice at the back of the carriage. "I bet she hasn't read them," he added. "She doesn't look like she's been on a lot of trains."

"He's right," confirmed Ellie, "I haven't."

The distraction technique worked. Barney agreed without argument and led Ellie down the aisle and to the safety instructions where they were comfortably out of earshot of their companions. Ray watched Barney use his hands in a far more animated way than he'd expected as the young man went through the safety instructions one by one. Ellie, in turn, proceeded to nod agreement, look concerned, giggle occasionally, but mostly follow Barney's narrative with a serious look on her face. Ray smiled at the little piece of theatre taking place at the end of the carriage. When he turned back in his seat, he saw that Elizabeth had been watching them and smiling too. "This is nice, isn't it?" he said. "We're becoming a proper little family."

"Humph!" snorted Elizabeth, dropping the smile from her face. "A dysfunctional family, perhaps."

"You can be the alcoholic single mother, if you like."

If the last comment was a feeble attempt at team building, it fell on deaf ears. If it was an attempt at humour, it failed even more dismally. Elizabeth still felt unsure; still felt claustrophobic. She usually felt much safer among strangers, but this odd collection of people had now become more than that. She knew their names. They were no longer anonymous. But they didn't know her name yet; she had made sure of that. Despite the sense of imminent danger that was keeping her from relaxing into the journey, something was stopping her from grabbing her bag and just running out of the carriage into another one where there might be more people; where there would be some strangers to get lost amongst. She didn't want to be intrigued by Ray or charmed by Barney; nor did she want to be amused by Ellie, but she had been drawn into the path of each one of them, and drawn in completely. She wasn't ready to admit that to this annoying man sitting opposite, so she looked for some kind of justification for still being there. It wasn't too difficult to think of a reason, mostly because it was honest. "I'm only staying because I want to keep an eye on Ellie," she said.

Ray shrugged. He hadn't asked the question that she seemed so adamant to answer. "That's fine with me," he said.

"It's true," insisted Elizabeth. "She's a lot more gullible than I am. Like I said, she was obviously never taught to be careful of strangers."

"Me neither," said Ray. Then he leaned in, looking the woman straight in the eyes, and added "lucky for you."

This didn't go down well at all. Elizabeth was the one who was supposed to be suspicious, not him. "What's that supposed to mean?" She bristled at the thought that she was the one to be careful of.

Ray sat back and his expression became more serious. Elizabeth wasn't sure if he was acting or not. It offended her either way. He folded his arms and spoke more firmly, more suspiciously, mirroring Elizabeth's own manner. "I'm taking you on trust, aren't I?" he said. "How do I know that *your* story was true, eh? You've been quick enough to judge me and Barney." His face took on a look of mock intrigue. He was enjoying himself so he pushed a little further. "You could be on the run for murder, for all we know."

It took Elizabeth a few seconds to work out what her response should be. To be affronted and walk off in a huff would be her usual reaction. How dare this man accuse her of being less than genuine, of being untrustworthy, when that was exactly what she was trying to do to him. However, he had got in first and that's what upset her. She decided she would play it cool. Like she told Ellie back in Cambridge, she could be anything she liked to anyone she liked because she would be out of their lives after four stations – or so she hoped. She didn't need to tell him any more than he needed to know. Elizabeth folded her arms, mirroring Ray right back at himself. She peered at him through half-closed eyes. This was her best attempt at looking inscrutable. It looked more like she was fighting back a sneeze. "That's right," she cooed, "for all you know I could be on a railway-themed killing spree."

To Elizabeth's dismay, Ray burst out laughing. Her attempt at being mysterious and sinister was simply juvenile and a little clumsy. He was clearly a better actor than she was. Of course he was; he was in the movie business. He'd been hanging around drama queens and kings all his life, not to mention all the actors. He shook his head with amusement. "No," he smirked, "I don't think so. People on the run tend to go in straight lines, not round and around in circles like you."

Ray decided to give Elizabeth a few moments to gather herself and come back at him – it was only fair – but, to his surprise, she didn't. Instead, she pressed her lips together tightly, as if she was struggling to keep in a word that was desperate to get out of her mouth. Ray could see that her cheeks were beginning to flush from the tension that was building up inside her. 'This isn't fun,' he thought to himself. 'If I'm not careful, this woman's going to burst into tears,' and that was something that, with all his self-confidence and assuredness, Ray was completely hopeless at dealing with… as he discovered once on location with Mabel Heep. He decided it would be better to get back to some safer ground and show Elizabeth that he was far more harmless than he looked. He unfolded his arms, took his jacket off and dropped it casually on Barney's empty seat. He reasoned to himself that this would somehow make him look less combative. It didn't really have the required effect. All it did was explain to Elizabeth why his expensive clothes looked so uncared for. "It's sweet," he said in a much friendlier tone, "that you want to look out for Ellie. She seems like a nice girl."

The tight lips relaxed a little and Elizabeth let out a sigh. "I'm sure she is a nice girl," she agreed, and a little of her tension subsided.

Ray's decision to move into neutral ground was working, so he moved in a bit further so that he could approach Elizabeth from a different angle. "And it says a lot about you that you'd want to look out for her like that. I mean," he added, "you hardly know her."

"The truth is," she explained, "I feel responsible for her now."

"How so?" asked Ray. He thought for a second that he might want to write some of this down. His hand moved unconsciously for the notebook in his pocket. Before he could pull it out, he stopped himself. 'That might just scare her,' he thought, so he put his hand on the table and pretended to brush away something that wasn't there.

"Well," admitted Elizabeth, "it's my fault, isn't it? If I hadn't told her about the seventh train, she'd be safely on her way to a nice little holiday by the sea instead of being stuck here with us."

"Ah," said Ray, because he just couldn't help himself. "It's *us* now, is it?" He wanted to laugh but instead he just smiled and reached out a hand to Elizabeth. "Welcome to the family, sister."

"I suppose that's better than being your alcoholic mother." Her eyes shone just a little at finding herself able to produce a witty riposte again, even if it was a small one. She reached out and gave Ray's hand a single, firm shake.

"A-ha!" cried Ray. "Did I see a little smile play across your lips then?"

That *was* what he saw. Elizabeth's mouth had indeed curled up at the corners. She shook her head self-consciously and the corners went back down until her lips were a horizontal line again. "You're looking too close," she said, but her eyes were still shining.

The soothing background clatter of the train on the tracks became loud and rattling and hollow as they hurtled into a tunnel. The strip lights in the carriage flickered for a moment and they both turned to look out of the window and into the dark. Ray checked out his reflection as it hovered before him in soft focus; any wrinkles and flaws smoothed as his mirror-self peered back. Elizabeth didn't enjoy hers nearly as much. The face reflected back at her looked blank and hard and joyless. She looked away from it in displeasure and studied Ray's reflection instead. He had taken his hat off and was smoothing down his hair. He looked at it from two different angles, decided it was beyond smoothing and replaced the hat on his head. He could feel Elizabeth's gaze on him as it bounced off the glass. 'It even works in reflections,' he thought, 'I can even feel other people's looks when they bounce off glass.' Window Ray flashed a smile at Window Elizabeth; the two of them suspended outside in the tunnel, beyond themselves. She didn't smile back at him. Instead, her cheeks flushed red and she looked away. She paused for a moment, trying to decide whether to front it out and glare at Ray for real, or whether to pretend to hunt in her bag for some imaginary item. Before she had time to do either, the train was out of the tunnel and Barney and Ellie were making their way back down the aisle.

"...and that's why you should always wipe the sink round afterwards." Barney's voice breached the awkwardness hanging around the table. He and Ellie were oblivious to any unease.

"I've always wondered about that," said Ellie.

"Yep," said Barney. "Most people don't even bother."

The older companions would never know exactly why the sink in a train, or anywhere else for that matter, should be wiped round afterwards. At least, according to Barney. They never got a chance to ask him. "I've taken Ellie through all the safety rules and regulations," he informed the party. "Maybe you two should think of reading them, especially if you're doing the seventh train."

"I don't get it," said Ray. "I thought you hated the rules. Isn't that why you started all this in the first place?"

He clearly hadn't explained himself earlier. Barney thought this man and woman were intelligent people. They certainly spoke as if they were. He would have to clarify. "I don't hate rules," he frowned with seriousness as he said it. "What I mean is, I don't hate them when they're in the right place. Do you see what I mean?"

Ellie was frowning now. "I'm not sure what you're talking about."

"Maybe I can help," interjected Ray.

Barney was having none of it. "No, no," he insisted. "I need to do it for myself."

Ray raised his hands in submission and relaxed back into his seat. Elizabeth forgot her own discomfort for a moment, leant forward and patted Barney's arm. "Go ahead, Barney."

The young man took a deep breath and spoke more carefully and with more consideration for the thoughts that were coming down from his brain and out of his mouth. He wasn't used to speaking like that, so the words came out more slowly than usual so that he could be sure he wanted to say them. "Some rules might not be right, but they're still rules until somebody changes them." He paused until the next thought had formed up fully in his head. The others waited. When he was ready, he gave a small nod to himself and continued. "That lovely, smooth grass in the park was just calling out for children to play all over it, but rules is rules, even if I don't agree with them anymore. Even if I think they're wrong." There was another brief pause while Barney made sure that the next bit was correct. "I don't want to break the rules, but maybe I can take my part of them away with me. Do you know what I mean?"

There was another pause before anyone attempted to answer the question that was hanging in the air. It might have sounded rhetorical, but it wasn't. Elizabeth nodded and patted Barney's arm again. Ray nodded, took out his notebook and scribbled a few words down. Ellie said, "I don't get it." Elizabeth moved her hand back to now pat Ellie on the arm, shushing her gently as she did so.

"What I'm trying to say," reiterated Barney, "is that I'm just trying to protect other people from myself."

"That's easy," said Ray with a snort. "What's difficult is protecting *yourself* from yourself." He still had the pen in his hand and he waggled it at Barney, beating out the last few syllables of his statement with it.

Barney blinked back at Ray blankly before he could speak again. He had never, ever thought his motives through to this extent. He was sure he had finished; satisfied with the last thing he said like he had never been satisfied with anything he'd said before. But now he had questions about it. "How do I do that?"

"Easy," said Ray. He put down his pen and turned in his seat towards Barney. He reached out his arms and grabbed the young man by the shoulders. Barney tensed and pulled back his head a little, not sure if this man was going to kiss him or punch him in the mouth. He would rather he did neither. Ray ignored the young man's obvious discomfort. "You do it by breaking the rules!" And with that, he released Barney, rubbed his hands together with satisfaction, and sat back in his seat like he was waiting for applause. To his dismay, none came.

Ellie leaned over towards Elizabeth. She meant to speak quietly but failed miserably. It came out in a loud whisper: "Are you following all this?" she asked her.

Elizabeth smiled. "Yes, I'm afraid I am."

"Will you explain it to me later?"

"I don't think so."

That wasn't the response that Ellie was expecting. She sat up and went back to her normal, proudly loud voice. "Why not?" she implored.

Elizabeth sighed. "Because, my dear girl, you don't need a cure for a disease you haven't got."

Ray's ears pricked up. "Hey," he said, "that's pretty good. Do you mind if I write that down?" He didn't wait for an answer. His pen was already moving across a fresh page in his notebook.

Before Ellie could ask somebody – anybody – to explain to her exactly what was going on, the woman with the perfect voice was ready to make her next announcement.

We will shortly be arriving at Kennett; Kennett is your next station stop. Please remember to collect all of your personal belongings when leaving the train.

"Three," said Ray with confidence.

"Three," said Elizabeth, reluctantly.

Ellie looked from one to the other and back again. Her confusion was forgotten. "Three," she said excitedly.

All three of them looked at Barney. He sunk a little in his seat. "Four," he said, almost inaudibly.

"Come on, Barney," urged Ray. "What are you going to do?"

"I don't know," said Barney. He sunk back even further into his seat, shaking his head.

"Three!" repeated Ellie. Her enthusiasm was increasing. It was so difficult to restrain that she'd began to bounce up and down in her seat. "Come with us, Barney, come on!"

"I don't know. I don't know," he wailed. His hand went to his mouth and he started nibbling furiously on a fingernail. "I think I need to go to the toilet." He rose from his seat and Ray pushed him down again. He fell back heavily.

The train began to slow and the sound of grinding brakes grew louder and louder. "The next station is drawing near," said Ray, his hand still on Barney's shoulder. "What are you going to do?"

"I don't know!" cried Barney. "It's really tough."

"Three! Three! Three!" Ellie clapped her hands as she called out the number.

Barney brushed Ray's hand off his shoulder. His strength took Ray by surprise and his hand fell back down more easily than he expected. His respect for the young man grew a little. Barney stood up from his seat and stepped into the aisle, wobbling with the lurching movement of the train as he did so. He steadied himself and spoke out, finding his voice. "Look," he said, "for three months I've been getting on the seventh train and counting four stops. This is *my* stop number four. We're coming up to number four."

"Three!" cried Ellie again. Elizabeth put her arm around the girl and squeezed her shoulder in an attempt to calm her down. It worked, but just a tiny bit. At least she stopped bouncing.

Barney was swaying from side to side. "Four stops. That's the rules. If I take away the rules, who am I?"

"Aha!" cried Ray in triumph. "Now there's a good question. Wouldn't you love to find out, Barney?" He leaned forward and rested his chin on his hands.

The train ground abruptly to a halt. Barney reached out his hand to grab the back of his now empty seat, missed, and landed sprawling on the floor.

The station is Kennett; Please remember to collect all of your personal belongings with you when leaving the train. Thank you for travelling with us today.

Ellie had reached out to grab Barney before he fell, but she was too late. Elizabeth and Ray were now standing and stretching over from their seats, trying to make sure that he hadn't hurt himself on the way down. Barney just lay there, curled into a little ball. Very softly, in a heart-wrenchingly melancholy way, he simply said: "Three."

"What did he say?" said Ray.

And then, a little louder but still with sadness in his voice, Barney repeated: "Three."

Ellie clapped her hands together with glee. "Three! He said 'three' – yay!"

Ray slid himself across Barney's seat, reached down to where his new friend was lying, and helped him gently back up to his feet. "Are you alright?" he asked in a fraternal tone. Barney nodded. "Good." There was no more to be said about that, so Ray moved back to his seat and made himself comfortable again.

"I have to go to the toilet," said Barney. He walked down the aisle with his head lowered, pulled open the door at the end, and walked through to the next carriage where the nearest toilet was to be found. He knew where it was because he'd seen the sign on the wall near the door when he first got on the train.

"You don't think he's going to get off here, do you?" asked Ellie with concern.

"No chance," said Ray. "His rucksack's still under the table. He wouldn't leave without that."

A moment later, a man and a woman got on the train, just before the doors closed. They glanced around the carriage, then made their way to another table at the opposite end to the others. They settled down next to each other. They looked like they were in their sixties and probably married. The woman took a flask and a package wrapped in tin foil out of her bag and placed them on the table. Then she motioned to the man to take off his hat, unwrapped the foil parcel and handed him a sandwich without saying anything.

Ellie had been peeking down the aisle, watching the little drama going on at the end. "Hey," she said. "Do you think they're doing the seventh train too?"

Ray and Elizabeth leaned over to take a look for themselves. The woman had taken out a book of crossword puzzles and passed it to her husband like he was a little boy who needed something to play with. As they munched on their sandwiches, she gazed out of the window, brushing crumbs of the table between mouthfuls. Neither of them said a word to each other. They were definitely married, and probably had been for a very long time.

"Nah," said Ray. "They're not Seventh Trainers. They're far too content."

Outside a whistle blew and the train chugged back to life. Elizabeth leaned back in her seat and rested her head on the glass of the window. The cool smoothness felt soothing on her skin. Kennett was a small village and there was just one, solitary passenger walking down the platform towards the station exit. Elizabeth wondered what it must be like to live in such a small community where everyone must know who you are and what you do. She suddenly missed the anonymity that she'd taken for granted for all those years in London. Despite the loneliness that it can bring, there's a certain safety in being invisible.

It was as if Ellie could read her mind. She nudged Elizabeth gently in the ribs. "Do you know what?" she said, which is always a strange question, because of course nobody knows what until the rest of that thought is expressed. "I don't even know your flippin' name."

This immediately piqued Ray's interest and he leant forward; uncomfortably close for Elizabeth. "That's right," he echoed, "we still don't know your name."

"Oh." There was no escape from it now. "It's…" She thought about lying for a moment, but what would be the point at this stage? "It's Elizabeth," she confessed.

"I'm very pleased to meet you Elizabeth." Ray reached out his hand towards her. Elizabeth reciprocated and reached hers towards him, expecting a firm, mocking handshake. Instead, he took it gently in his and kissed the back of her hand.

This little gesture of chivalry took Elizabeth by surprise. It was playful but not mocking at all. It had a curiously calming effect on her and she relaxed a little. She took back her hand and offered Ray a friendly smile. "Elizabeth," she repeated. "I haven't said that out loud for weeks." Ray smiled back and they held each other's gazes for a moment until Ellie intervened.

"It's funny. I had you down as a Margaret."

"Margaret? Really?" Elizabeth wasn't sure how to take this.

"Yeah," said Ellie. She saw the disappointed look on Elizabeth's face and felt the need to reassure her. "I meant it nicely," she said. "Margaret is my gran's name. I love my gran," she added wistfully.

Welcome aboard this Greater Anglia rail service for Ipswich, calling at Bury St Edmunds, Stowmarket and Ipswich. Thank you for travelling with us today.

"Woo-hoo!" Ellie's exuberance returned. "Bury St Edmunds here we come! I still don't flippin' know where that is."

"It's another stop on the journey," said Ray philosophically. "Just another part of the marvellous middle."

The door opened and then closed with a clunk at the far end of the carriage. Ellie leaned out from her seat into the aisle and was pleased to see Barney making his way back towards them. He paused when he reached the table and apologised to the others before sitting back down. He was roundly assured by everyone that there was nothing to apologise for. He did it again anyway.

"As long as you're OK, Barney," said Elizabeth. She smiled reassuringly.

Barney was visibly shaken and his cheeks had grown pale. His hair was a little bit wet just behind his ears where he'd obviously been splashing water on his face. He shook his head. "I don't know," he said. "I'm still on the train, aren't I?" He put his head in his hands and sighed. "I just broke the rules, didn't I?"

Elizabeth smiled. "I'm afraid so." Despite all her reservations, she'd really warmed to her youthful companions. They both had a certain innocence and openness to the world that she'd forgotten could exist in young people today. There were no children in her life and she rarely had either the desire or occasion to converse with anyone under the age of twenty-five, apart from when they were serving her in coffee shops, of course. Most of the youths she'd come across on her train journeys had been arrogant, loud, over-confident, often frightening, or sometimes just plain drunk, or worse. At least, that's what she'd come to believe. She began to think that she'd dismissed a whole generation without ever really speaking to them, let alone listening to what they had to say. So many assumptions were being challenged today.

"Well then," shrugged Barney, "I guess anything could happen now. That's a bit scary."

"The world is your lobster!" cried Ellie triumphantly.

Barney lifted his head and smiled a proper wide smile. It was the only time the others had seen him do so and they all noticed, for the first time, that there were dimples in his cheeks when he grinned. "I like lobsters," he said.

"Is Bury St Edmunds by the seaside?" asked Ellie.

"No, I don't think so," replied Ray.

"Oh, that's a shame," said Ellie.

Chapter Ten:
Bury St Edmunds Station

This is a customer safety announcement. Please be sure to keep personal belongings with you at all times and report any suspicious activity to staff at the station security office. Thank you for travelling with us today.

It was that same female voice that they used at all the stations on this rail network. The same, polite safety announcement over and over again. Elizabeth found it reassuringly familiar. Sometimes, when she was over-tired, she would thank the perfect voice out loud from whichever platform at whatever station she happened to be at. But only when she thought nobody else was listening.

As the four, accidental travelling companions gathered their personal belongings around themselves, Ellie called out, "Thank you," to the perfect voice. Elizabeth was astonished. That was the second time that Ellie appeared to read her thoughts. Was it a coincidence? She stared at the girl, eyebrows raised and mouth open. "What?" asked Ellie innocently. "I was only being polite."

"You do know it's a recording, don't you?" said Barney. He didn't want to assume, but he wasn't entirely sure whether Ellie understood or not. She was, after all, new to all this.

"Duh!" she exclaimed, by way of confirming, in a word, that she did indeed understand. "I know it's a recording, but it's a recording of a real person, silly." There was nothing that Barney could think of to say to that.

The platform was quiet. Just a handful of passengers were waiting for the next train, some sitting, some standing, no-one talking at all, except for Ellie who was chattering away to Ray like a budgie with a new mirror.

Bury St Edmunds station is small and well-ordered. Just two platforms and two tracks running neatly parallel and off into the long, flat Suffolk countryside. Stern, square, wooden troughs housed displays of multi-coloured plants and flowers, cheerfully blooming despite their austere housing. Barney stooped to feel the leaves between his fingers. He was happy to see that someone had taken such care over the plants. There wasn't a weed in sight. Elizabeth caught his eye and smiled, and he called her over so that he could point out all the different heathers and cyclamens, in case she didn't know what they were called.

As Ellie wittered on in her cheerful way, Ray pretended to listen, as he surveyed his new surroundings. Huddled around the station was a jumble of mismatched warehouses and small industrial buildings, mostly unloved and semi-derelict, while in the background, looming over all of it, stood one of the town's most notable landmarks – the sugar factory, pumping out milk-white steam into the cold, winter air. 'Bury St Edmunds sounded prettier than it looks,' thought Ray.

Taken all together for the first time, the scene greeting new arrivals at the station is deceptive. It hides what lies beyond very successfully. It's as if the townsfolk had got together a century and a half before and decided to make the first glimpse of their home as ugly as possible so that visitors arriving by rail – or road, for that matter, because the view from the A14 is just as bad – would turn up their noses and travel straight through to somewhere else. In truth, a short walk into the centre exposes a very attractive market town, full of history and charm and coffee shops. The Seventh Trainers would soon discover this.

"Right then." Ray clapped his hands to get everyone's attention. "What do you all say we take a break from the trains and go and find some lunch in town?" No-one jumped in with an answer straight away. "Come on," urged Ray. "I'm buying."

There was a lot to take in, and much to think about. None of this was planned. Not one of the intrepid wanderers had foreseen that they would be travelling in a group by now. Elizabeth, for one, hadn't expected this at any stage. But it was cold and an icy wind was blowing straight down the platform and whipping at everyone's hands and faces. Ellie responded first: "I'm up for it, Ray. I've never been to Bury St Edmunds before, have you?"

"Nope. I don't think any of us have. What about you?"

Elizabeth shook her head. Barney shrugged. "I *am* hungry," he admitted. "And if you mean it when you say you're buying…"

"That's settled then." Ray was in no mood to dither. "Let's go."

Outside the station, Barney found a local map on the wall and insisted that everyone wait while he had a good look and got his bearings. "It's this way," he asserted, once he was finally happy that he'd read the whole map, and he led the motley crew out of the station car park and down towards the town. Being the young gentleman that he was, he even offered to drag Ellie's overstuffed suitcase so that she didn't have to. That pleased her enormously and freed her up to chatter some more without getting out of breath as they walked.

Past modern apartment blocks, Victorian terraces, Georgian townhouses, and medieval cottages they walked until the four found themselves in the town's historic market square. It was Wednesday, and the square was full of people and stalls selling all kinds of wares from the most useful to the highly frivolous. "Ooh!" cried Ellie. "It didn't look anything like this from the station," she said, quite rightly. "Can we stop and do a bit of shopping?"

"Do what you like," said Ray. "I'm going to look for somewhere to eat, I'm starving," and his stomach led him on, weaving in and out of shoppers and stalls like a man on a mission. Barney was right behind him, dragging the suitcase along with some difficulty as he struggled to keep up. His stomach was rumbling too.

"Come on, Ellie." Elizabeth took the girl's hand and pulled her along behind the men. Ellie allowed herself to be towed reluctantly, craning her head round from one side to the other to eye up the eclectic mix of stalls and shops as they went. It wasn't until she'd accidentally mowed down an angry shopper that she grudgingly agreed to look where she was going, but only after she'd been told off by Elizabeth and sworn at by the shopper

Just off the main market square was Abbeygate Street; a characterful thoroughfare with more than its fair share of eateries. "This will do," asserted Ray, as he strode into the first one that looked not too cheap and not too full.

Barney followed, tugging the suitcase noisily over the stone threshold.

Elizabeth and Ellie got to the corner of the street just in time to see Ray and Barney disappearing into the selected restaurant. A second later and they would have lost them. The women stopped briefly to read the menu in the silver-coloured frame on the wall outside. "I hope Ray meant it when he said he'd pay," said Elizabeth after checking the prices on display.

The cost wasn't bothering Ellie. She still had all her holiday spending money tucked into her purse. "Yep, I can eat in here," she said. "I'm a vegetarian."

"Oh," said Elizabeth. She wasn't surprised by this at all. Then they both stepped into the restaurant and made their way to a table for four by the window where Ray and Barney were already perusing the large, deliberately rustic-looking menu.

The dishes on offer were suitably metropolitan, with the likes of halloumi fries and various foam garnishes available. Ray was impressed. He had previously made up his mind that Suffolk was some rural backwater devoid of hummus. Now he was happy to be proved wrong. Mostly because he was famished.

It was now getting on for three o'clock but the restaurant was still surprisingly busy. Market day shoppers and 'ladies who lunch' were tucking into home-made fish finger sandwiches and glasses of Merlot at fashionably distressed wooden tables. Ellie was asking Ray a series of questions about Bury St Edmunds that he couldn't answer, but he was giving them a go anyway. Barney was busy wolfing down a plate of steak, chips and mushrooms with peppercorn sauce, after checking and re-checking that Ray was definitely happy to pay for his meal. Barney stopped asking when he received the reply: "Ask me one more time and you can pay for your own – and mine."

Elizabeth sat back and watched it all going on around her. Her initial misgivings were receding, but everything still felt strange. She'd had no intention of taking up with other travellers – quite the opposite – yet here she was having lunch with three strangers as if it were the most natural thing in the world. That was the strange bit; that it all felt so normal. She liked Ellie all the way back at Cambridge station, almost from the moment she'd sat down with that ridiculous suitcase. Was that really only a couple of hours ago? So much had changed. And Barney seemed like a genuinely decent young man. A bit naive, perhaps, but harmless and certainly a gentle soul. There was nothing to fear from him, she thought. And then there was Ray. She still hadn't quite worked him out. That would take a bit longer. She loved those films he talked about. Was that really him? She couldn't even check her facts online without a phone. But why would he lie? She'd pretended to be a hotel inspector, an art collector – what if Ray was just doing the same thing? No, that didn't make sense. He certainly seemed to have money, although the bill hadn't come yet. If he did pay, what would that prove? And if he didn't…

"Is your food okay?" Ray's question snapped Elizabeth out of her musings.

"Oh, yes, it's fine. Thank you."

"It's just that you're not eating."

Elizabeth picked up her cutlery and prodded at the food on her plate. "I was just thinking, that's all." Before she could voice exactly what she was thinking, Ellie cut in. Elizabeth was fine with that.

"Oh yeah, that's what I meant to ask you all," said Ellie. "Why is it seven trains and not six or nine?"

"Ah, that's simple." Ray answered without hesitation. He put down his knife and waved his fork around for emphasis as he spoke, prodding it into the air at particular moments. "I've thought about this a lot. Because you're right, it could have been five or twelve..."

"Or nine," interrupted Barney with a mouth half full of mushrooms.

"You shouldn't speak with your mouth full," chided Ellie.

"Sorry," spluttered Barney, and three mushrooms fell out of the side of his mouth and into his lap. He brushed them onto the floor in the hope that no-one had noticed.

"Indeed," continued Ray undeterred. "When I first got into films seriously – as a career, I mean – I noticed that almost all of my favourite movies had the number seven in the title."

"Like what?" asked Ellie.

"Oh, just off the top of my head, *The Seventh Seal, The Seven Faces of Dr Lao, The Seven Samurai...*"

"*The Magnificent Seven*," added Barney, the mushrooms first having been swallowed this time.

"That's the same movie, actually," Ray informed him.

"Is it?" Barney looked perplexed. "Are you sure?"

"Absolutely," assured Ray. "Different country, same story. Japan versus Hollywood. Take your pick."

Barney looked adequately impressed and paused from eating as he tried to think of some more examples.

In the meantime, Elizabeth was finding the new turn in the conversation intriguing, despite herself, and joined in with a couple of suggestions of her own: "*The Seven Year Itch*. Oh, and *Seven Brides for Seven Brothers*," she offered.

"Both classics of their genre," said Ray approvingly.

"Oh, oh!" squeaked Ellie, finally finding an example of her own. "*Snow White and the Seven Dwarves*. I love that film," and she sat back in her chair gazing upwards with a grin, as if it were being screened right now on the ceiling for her pleasure.

"Indeed," agreed Ray with a smile. "And then, last but by no means least, there's *Se7en*."

"Seven what?" asked Barney and Ellie at exactly the same time. They looked at each other, cried, "Jinks!" simultaneously, then both burst into childlike peals of laughter.

Ray waited patiently for the hilarity to die down before elucidating. "Just *Se7en*." The other three looked puzzled. Ray tried again. "You know, Brad Pitt and Morgan Freeman…*Se7en*."

The penny dropped and they all said 'Oh, right,' in chorus. "That was a strange film," added Barney.

"Anyway," continued Ray, putting down his fork and resting his elbows on the table, "in answer to your original question, Ellie, I guess I've always been inspired by films with the number seven in the title and this…" he waved his hands around himself for dramatic emphasis, "what I'm doing is my own offering, if you like. I'm writing my own 'Seven' movie with every train I get on."

"You really have thought this through," said Elizabeth.

"I have indeed," said Ray, "although, I must admit, I didn't work it out until after I get on that first train in Paddington." He shoved the last morsel of truffle-oil-covered food into his mouth, picked up his napkin, wiped his mouth and leaned back in his chair, satiated.

Without allowing anyone time to pause and marvel at Ray's knowledge of film – which he would very much have enjoyed – Ellie moved straight on. "What about you, Barney?" Ray was a little miffed, but had to concede that he too was interested in the young man's take on things. Elizabeth was equally keen to hear what he had to say.

Barney pushed a few chips onto his fork with his knife, stuffed them in his mouth, and chewed for a moment to give himself time to consider the question. He made sure his mouth was empty this time before speaking. "I'm just thinking," he said. "Give me a minute." Then he waited for everyone to complete their meals and put down their cutlery out of politeness, although he already knew what he was going to say before they'd all finished. "It's always been my favourite number. Have you ever heard of 'the seventh wave?'" He offered the question to the table generally.

Ellie answered first. "Is that like a 'surfer dude' thing?"

Barney considered for a moment. "No... Well, sort of."

"I know what it is," said Ray.

Elizabeth stopped him. "Let him finish."

Ray yielded and Barney continued. "There's this theory," he said, "that waves move in patterns across the oceans and then wash up on the seashore in sevens." He nodded as if to check what he was saying was right. He was happy with it. "I read it in a book. Apparently, the seventh wave is always the biggest. So, if you sit on the beach and watch carefully for long enough, you can count them."

"Really?" said Ellie, genuinely intrigued.

"Yep," assured Barney.

"That's right," confirmed Ray, although he really didn't have to. He just enjoyed doing it.

"Mind you," said Barney, "I've never tried it, but I'd like to one day. Yeah, I like the idea of being able to know in advance which wave I should look out for."

"Which one you need to run away from, you mean." Elizabeth hadn't meant to say that out loud, but it just came out. All of these little comments were revealing more about her and her state of mind than she intended. They were clues for the others to pick up, if they'd noticed. She blushed.

Barney hadn't read anything into what Elizabeth said. Maybe Ray had, but Barney tended to take everyone on face value. His reply was guileless and simple, at least for him. "It depends," said Barney. "Some people see a big wave and run away, some people run towards it so they can ride on the top."

"That's really flippin' cool!" grinned Ellie. "If I do get to Brighton one day, I'm going to sit on the beach, count the waves and think of you, Barney."

It was now Barney's turn to blush a little. "Who knows," he said, casting a coy sideways glance at Ellie, "I might end up there myself and count them with you."

Ellie beamed back at him. Elizabeth glanced affectionately from one to the other and back again. Maybe there was something blossoming between these two. It was sweet. It was the kind of thing that would normally bring out the cynic in her. In a matter of seconds, her mind raced through flashing images of all her failed relationships in chronological order, punctuated by all the dry spinsterhood in between, right back to her teenage years when she still had hopes of finding happiness. The images came to a halt and there she was: a single, middle-aged woman sitting at a restaurant table opposite two young people with all their hopes intact and all their futures not yet broken. She sat back in her chair, pushed back by the weight of envy that rushed into her. It was unexpected, and a shock to discover that she was a jealous person and hadn't known it. Elizabeth dropped her hands down by her sides. She imagined the envy flowing down from her head and chest to seep out of her fingers and onto the floor. She didn't want it in her. None of the others seemed to notice, which was fortunate.

"So," said Ellie, turning her attention away from Barney to Elizabeth. "What about you, Liz?"

For the first time ever, she didn't mind being called Liz. Maybe it was because Ellie had said it. Elizabeth shook out her hands and rested them back on the table. The envy had subsided.

"Come on," urged Ellie. "Don't keep us in flippin' suspense."

"Do you know," mused Elizabeth, "I have absolutely no idea how or why I decided it would be the seventh train. I just did. It just seemed… I don't know, the right number. It could just as easily have been eight."

"But it wasn't," asserted Ray.

Elizabeth shrugged, as if to say it was the best explanation she had. "It's ridiculous, now that I think about it, but that's just how it happened."

The next ten minutes passed while Ray proceeded to illuminate Elizabeth about her motives and she proceeded to fold her arms and shake her head in denial. He loved a challenge, but this was going nowhere. A polite intrusion from a waitress was welcomed by all, including Ray, and as plates were cleared away and coffees were ordered, attention was turned to Ellie.

"So, tell me, lobster girl," said Ray amiably. "Now that you're a Seventh Trainer like us, don't you think it's your turn to tell your story?" Ellie considered this for a moment then held her empty hands out in front of her, as if to show she had nothing. "Come on," pressed Ray, "everybody's got a story."

"Have they?" Elizabeth stressed the words in an attempt to shield the girl from the kind of questioning she'd been subjected to, amiable or otherwise. Ray and Barney both insisted that those were the rules and everyone had to share and that's just how it was, while Elizabeth resisted.

Ellie was the only one who didn't join in the debate. She felt no pressure at all. She was enjoying the whole adventure more than anyone else. This was all part of the journey. "All right, all right," she interjected. The others stopped, all appeased in their own way. "I'll tell you my story, but it's pretty boring."

"That's for us to judge," said Ray.

"Let her speak," cut in Elizabeth. Ray mimed the zipping of his mouth then held up a hand in surrender. No-one expected that mouth to stay zipped for very long, but it was nice while it lasted.

"Well," continued Ellie, "I work part-time in *John Lewis* – glass and crockery – and then the rest of the time I'm at Uni in Cambridge."

"Cambridge," said Ray, clearly impressed. Elizabeth rolled her eyes at his freshly unzipped mouth and he covered it with his hand. "Sorry," he mumbled through his fingers.

"Yeah, Cambridge. It's nice."

"What are you studying?" asked Elizabeth. "If you don't mind me asking."

"I'm doing a Masters in Theoretical Physics," replied Ellie with simple casualness. The other three froze, staring at the girl with various expressions of bafflement on their faces. If they still had cutlery in their hands, they would have dropped them noisily. Ray opened his mouth to comment but quickly closed it again. He had nothing to say. Nor did anyone else at that moment, except for Ellie. "It's only part-time," she explained, as if that would make it easier to accept.

As if with one voice, Ray and Barney simply said "Wow!" in perfect harmony.

"Yeah," agreed Ellie. "Everybody reacts like that."

"Well," conceded Elizabeth, "I wasn't expecting that. I'm afraid I've misjudged you, my girl."

"That's alright. I reckon we all do that a bit too much. Flippin' shame, ain't it?" Ellie smiled and put out her hand. Elizabeth covered it with her own hand and squeezed.

Four hot drinks of different kinds arrived just then, via the waitress and a large tray: a hot chocolate with whipped cream and marshmallows for Ellie, a black coffee for Elizabeth, a caramel latte for Barney, and a double espresso for Ray.

Ellie picked up the spoon from her saucer and stirred the long glass with relish until all the pink and white marshmallows began to melt into the steaming chocolate.

"D'you know what?" she exclaimed, not actually expecting an answer, "It's just flippin' hit me. If there hadn't been a spare chair at your table in the coffee shop in Cambridge, I'd be halfway to boring Brighton right now and I wouldn't be sitting here with you."

"Nor would I." Elizabeth thought about where she might be now. Perhaps on another train heading to a different town. She pictured herself in some railway station café, sitting alone with a black coffee, waiting for the seventh train to be announced; reading a bit of her book, watching the world go by and imagining what kind of lives all the strangers around her were living. Wherever else she could have been at this moment, she was sure there wouldn't have been anyone else sharing the journey. It occurred to her that, for the past month, she had been lonely – but she hadn't realised it until now. That was precisely what she'd been running away from, and yet it had travelled with her on every train and through every station. It was only today, in the absence of that loneliness, that she noticed it.

"Spooky, isn't it?" said Ellie. "I'm really glad there was a spare chair, aren't you?"

Elizabeth squeezed Ellie's hand again. "I am now."

"Me too," said Barney.

"Me too," said Ray. His voice was warmer, softened by a smile as he spoke. He meant it, and Elizabeth could finally believe him.

True to his word, Ray paid the bill plus a generous tip with a flash of his credit card. The conversation relaxed and continued with new-found friendliness as hot drinks were drained and it was time to go. Time was ticking on and the four still had journeys to make.

Outside, it was getting dark as the weak winter sun slid down behind the day. Barney led the walk back to the station, dragging the big suitcase behind him, with all of them having to stop and wait here and there while Ellie perused market stalls and squealed at various shiny objects in shoe shop windows like a baby magpie.

It was after four o'clock when they walked up the steps and back on to platform two at Bury St Edmunds station. They didn't know how long they might have to wait for the seventh train, or which platform it might leave from, but the only waiting room was on that side. So, after much debating downstairs, they agreed to be ready to run back down and up the steps to the other side if necessary.

As the winter sky darkened, the chill wind got colder and the prospect of standing around outside for too long wasn't appealing. A handful of passengers were waiting on the opposite platform. The day's throng of commuters hadn't yet arrived to catch their train home and schoolchildren and college students had already gone. A single male traveller was waiting at the far end of platform two, while a young couple cuddled up on a bench at the opposite end as far away as possible from any eyes that might want to pry into their stolen moments of intimacy.

"Where are we gonna end up next?" wondered Ellie out loud. "The world is our flippin' lobster, ain't it?"

The next train to arrive at platform two is the sixteen-twenty-six service to Ipswich, calling at Thurston, Elmswell, Stowmarket, Needham Market and Ipswich. Platform two for the next service to Ipswich.

"One!" cried Ellie triumphantly. Ray laughed and echoed the cry. Barney joined in without the need for any persuasion at all. Elizabeth did the same after a little cajoling, but not quite as loud. The next part of the journey had begun. In the distance, the train to Ipswich was approaching and the tracks began their familiar low rattle, growing steadily louder and louder.

"Come on," said Elizabeth. "Shall we get inside that waiting room. My feet are freezing." The others keenly agreed.

Ellie's suitcase was still in Barney's hands as he wrestled to turn its wheels towards the waiting room door. All of a sudden, he let out an ear-splitting roar and the suitcase crashed to the ground with a hefty thump, followed by his rucksack. Before the others had a chance to react, Barney was racing down the platform towards the far end where the single male passenger had been standing. Ray responded first, setting off at a sprint behind Barney. The younger man was faster and fitter and Ray struggled to catch him. Ellie managed to manoeuvre the suitcase back on its feet with difficulty, grabbed Barney's rucksack, then headed off towards the two men as fast as she could, Elizabeth following behind with her own bags flapping around her.

By the time Ray reached the end of the platform, Barney was lying on top of a sprawling stranger shouting, "Behind the yellow line! Behind the yellow line!" as the train pulled heavily into the station beside them. At the other end of the platform, the young couple craned their necks to see what was going on, decided it was none of their business, and got on the train as soon as the doors opened.

The stranger was flat on his back on the ground, eyes wide, breathing heavily, staring without emotion at the wooden roof of the station platform. Ray pulled Barney off the man and roughly back onto his feet, apologising profusely for his young companion's over-zealousness with trackside safety regulations. By this time, Ellie had arrived at the bizarre scene with Elizabeth puffing loudly a few paces behind her. "Barney!" yelled Elizabeth. "What have you done?"

The man was still lying on the floor, dazed and winded from the weight of a crazy guy hitting him full in the chest. "He was over the yellow line!" howled Barney, breathing hard.

"Dear God, it doesn't matter," said Elizabeth, catching her breath.

"Yes, it does, it does," said Barney. "He was going to jump!"

"No way!" cried Ellie. "Is that true?" She crouched down to look at the man more closely. "Were you going to jump?"

All four of them stared down at the stranger on the ground, who was groaning now and rubbing his chest. Ray put out a hand to help him up from the floor. The man took it and pulled himself back onto his feet, swaying a little when he got there. He looked at each of them in turn, eyes wide and staring, then suddenly crumpled back down to the ground and burst into tears.

"Help him," urged Elizabeth. "Let's get him into the waiting room." Taking hold of one arm each, Ray and Barney carefully helped the man back up to a standing position and walked him down the platform to the waiting room. Luckily, it was empty. A low, black, vinyl couch stood against the back wall and the two men gently lowered the stranger down on to it. He was still sobbing. "Ellie, go and get him a cup of tea from the café. And put lots of sugar in it," instructed Elizabeth. Ellie parked her suitcase next to the couch and ran off to fetch the tea. Elizabeth sat next to the man and took his hand. It was trembling. "It's OK," she assured him. "You're not alone."

Thoughts of Chalk Farm tube station flooded through Elizabeth's mind and the words she was saying out loud were echoing around her head. These were the words she had been waiting to hear since that day exactly four weeks ago: 'You're not alone.' She hadn't expected them to come from her own lips. She opened her handbag and fished around for a tissue, found one, and handed it to the man.

"Thank you," he said, his voice wobbling as he fought to hold back more tears. Then he turned to Barney. "You saved my life. Thank you."

Barney said nothing. He just nodded and smiled. Ray patted his young companion on the shoulder with new-found respect, then sat down to join Elizabeth and the stranger on the couch. "What's your name, my friend?" he asked gently.

"Daniel," said the man.

"I'm Ray. This is Elizabeth. Ellie's just gone to fetch you a cup of tea, and our young hero here is called Barney."

The man nodded the best greeting he could manage under the circumstances, blew his nose hard and put the soiled tissue into his pocket. "I'm so sorry," he said, rubbing his eyes with the back of his hand. "I made you miss your train."

"No, you didn't," chirped Barney. "That was only the first train. We've got six more to go."

The man looked baffled. Elizabeth patted his hand. "Don't worry," she reassured him. "Barney just means that we've got some time before our train comes, that's all. We've got all the time you need."

The waiting room door opened heavily. A tall, wide man wearing a woolly hat walked in, took a quick look around, decided that it all looked a bit intense in there, and hurriedly walked back out onto the platform. He pulled his dark jacket around him more tightly and glanced back round over his shoulder. Elizabeth watched him through the glass door. The man noticed, and shuffled along the platform until he was out of sight.

The waiting room door opened again and Ellie breezed in with a cup full of hot, sweet tea. "Here you go." She passed it to the man, then sat on the arm of the couch next to Elizabeth. "So, what's going on?" she enquired in all innocence. "Was he really trying to kill himself?"

"Ellie!" Elizabeth nudged the girl in the ribs. Ellie let out a high-pitched yelp and then apologised for any offence that her frankness might have caused.

"No, *I'm* sorry," said the man, this time directly to Ellie. "I'm so, so sorry."

"Have a sip of tea," suggested Elizabeth. "It will make you feel better."

"You're not hurt or anything, are you?" asked Ray. "Nothing broken? Barney mowed you down like a… well, like a…"

The man completed the sentence to save Ray from his awkward stumbling. "Like a train?"

185

A short snort of laughter burst from Ellie's lips. She apologised again. The man smiled, then laughed himself. It was the contradiction of it all, like people who can't stop giggling at funerals. Barney let out a long breath and his shoulders relaxed for the first time since he'd rugby-tackled the stranger to the ground. He sat down on a second couch that stood next to the first one against the wall, shorter and harder and mismatched. He looked at the man thoughtfully. "Did I really save your life?"

"Yes, I think you did. I was way too close to the edge. I could easily have been pulled down." The man took a sip of his tea and leaned back, easing his shoulders into the couch. "Where are you all going?"

There was a pause. The other four glanced at each other, not knowing quite how to explain their travel arrangements. Ellie decided to just say it. "We don't know where we're going yet."

This gave Barney the courage to add some more. "We're all doing the seventh train."

The man looked bemused and leaned forward again, spilling a little hot tea into his lap in the process. He brushed it off. "The seventh train? What's that?"

"Never mind," interjected Elizabeth. "You just sit here as long as you need to. You've had a shock. Is there anyone we can call for you?"

"No," the man shook his head. "I'll be fine. If you all need to go…"

"Not a problem," assured Ray. "We've got all the time in the world."

"If you need to talk…" said Elizabeth.

She didn't have a chance to finish the sentence. The man *did* want to talk. He had to. There was so much going on inside his head that he felt like he was about to burst. He took a deep breath. "My name's Daniel Cotter, and I'm a train driver," he began.

Chapter Eleven:
The Last Train from Harlow Town Station

My dad was a good man. I see so many young boys out there, from the same place where I grew up, who don't have that in their lives. I see them getting into trouble, finding their way into bad places with bad people, just because they've got no decent role models to look up to. I was lucky. My dad was a good man and I can't blame him for anything.

At school I was pretty average at everything except football and physics. I don't know how or why I was put together to excel at those two things in particular, but there it is. I bet Ronaldo don't care too much about the Theory of Relativity. For some reason, I totally got physics. It made sense to me and I liked it. It explained how everything worked. I had a great left foot on the football pitch too. My parents were never disappointed that I got no more than a 'C' in anything else, but in physics it was 'A' all the way. Maybe that's why they went easy on me for the rest. Problem was, even if I wanted to go to some university or other, it was no good without the Maths and the English, and no matter how hard I tried, I never got better than a lazy average in either of them. As for football, I had the feet but I didn't have the heart. It's no use without the passion, and that's just how it is. I did play in the local Sunday league for a couple of seasons, just for fun. My old man came to watch every single match.

Some days I do wonder where I would be now if I'd have made it to university, sitting in them science labs and lecture halls with all the other brains. I would have been the first one in my family to get there. It would have been good. Perhaps I wouldn't be sitting in the waiting room of Bury St Edmunds station right now if I'd have tried a bit harder at school. Come to think of it, there's no perhaps about it.

So, the time came for school to be done and for me to pick a path. I didn't take too long thinking about it. I went to dad and told him that I wanted to go and work on the railways, just like him, and just like his father before him. I don't think I ever saw the old man look so proud. All the time I was growing up, I never once saw my father cry, but I could swear there was a tear in his eye that day. It was him that helped me get the job and told me what I should say at the interview and how to conduct myself properly. Of course, I got the job. On my very first morning, dad got up early and made two ham and tomato sandwiches and put them in a lunch box that he'd asked my mum to go out and buy as a surprise for me. He wouldn't let her make them, even though she tried to chase him out of her kitchen. Nope, he wanted to do it himself. I ate them in my lunch break. There was too much salt on the tomato, just the way dad liked it himself. I ate them anyway.

My father died six months after I completed my driver training. It was the lung cancer. They all smoked back then, even on the trains. He was fifty-four years old. Never made it all the way to retirement like his dad did. My mum made my sandwiches after that. Always ham and tomato with too much salt. We never spoke about changing what went into my lunchbox and I never complained. Sometimes I ate them, sometimes I gave them away, but the box was always empty when I got home. Mum always checked. She had her own peculiar ways of dealing with loss. Women are smart like that.

It was a full ten years more before I killed a man. By then I had my own flat, just a few streets away from mum so I was there if she needed me, but I was making my own sandwiches. We know that these things happen. It's part of our training when we become drivers. There's a whole section in the manual about what to do when a person steps out in front of your train, but nothing – and I mean nothing – prepares you for it. I knew other drivers that it happened to. Everybody copes differently. One guy at my depot was back at work the very next day, calm and accepting, but they wouldn't let him get back behind the wheel for a week. Another guy went home and never came back, after a young girl stepped in front of his train. Like I said, everybody copes differently.

My father drove a train for more than thirty years. My grandfather was a driver even longer. All those years combined, and it never once happened to either of them. Maybe they were lucky, or maybe it's just the times that we're living in now. Some people fall onto the tracks and get killed by accident. It's always tragic, sometimes stupid, but it happens. The ones who do it on purpose are mostly men, and plenty of them are younger than me.

I thought I would be able to handle it with logic and science. I know exactly how long it takes a moving train to come to a stop, depending on how fast it's travelling. I know how much weight and how much force is behind a train that hits something on the tracks that shouldn't be there. It's all physics. But absolutely nothing prepares you for the sight and the sound and the feeling of hitting a human being with the train that you happen to be driving; the thing that you're in charge of.

I saw his face. I will never forget it as long as I live. He looked no more than twenty years old with dark hair and dark eyes. There was no expression on that face. Nothing. His eyes were wide open and he held his arms straight out to the side like some suicide Jesus. I did all the things we're trained to do. I alerted the guard and stopped any other trains coming. I called the emergency services and the transport police and made the report like I was on autopilot. It takes time to sort out something like that. There are all kinds of checks and double-checks to do, and everything has to be written down. It was a couple of hours before it was all done and finished and the undertakers had come to take him away in a plain box. The boss got someone to give me a lift home and told me to take some time off, as long as I needed, and said that he'd call me the next day. I went straight round to see my mum, just like I did when I was a little boy and got into some trouble or other. It was only when I was sat down in the kitchen with her that I started shaking and crying. Delayed shock. That's what it's like. Mum told me I should go upstairs to my old room and stay the night. I ended up staying for a week.

Seven days of home cooking, some good sleep, and a lot of applied logic, and I was ready to go back to work. Sometimes it's a real blessing to have a brain that understands things with science. It wasn't my fault that my train hit that sad man. It could have been any train. It just happened to be mine. It was dreadful, and I really felt bad for the guy and whatever family he left behind, but I reasoned to myself that he was killed by the train and not by the driver. There was absolutely nothing I could have done to stop it. The brakes went on the second I saw him, I knew that for sure. I went over it in my head a thousand times.

When I got back to the depot, my boss had a good, long talk with me about the whole thing and then agreed I should get back behind the wheel as soon as possible. He gave me the option of moving to a different kind of job within the company, but I thought about what my dad would have done in my place. He would have carried on. He would have been strong. My grandad would have done exactly the same thing, although he would probably have been driving the very next day. My grandad was made of steel, like all the other old Jamaican boys that used to drink with him in the Railway Arms on Friday nights.

So, I got straight back on the horse, so to speak. The first journey was tense. I had to talk to myself out loud the whole way. I don't think I've ever been more alert in my whole life. My pulse was racing the whole way from Liverpool Street to Hertford East, but I made it safe and sound. The next journey was a bit easier. The next journey was easier still. After a few weeks, everything was pretty much back to normal. It's not that you can forget something like that when it happens to you, I don't think that's possible, but you learn to ride with it. You take a little bit more care, and you get a little more philosophical about life, but normality creeps back in eventually and the memory of it shrinks until you can tuck it away somewhere safe.

Two more years passed, and by then I'd moved to a slightly bigger flat. I needed the extra space because I'd met Paula. I don't mean to brag – that's not my style – but a lot of women had come and gone in my bachelor days. Paula was the one that stuck. She was a teacher in a local secondary school and she was as smart as she was good looking. She'd done all the studying and the university stuff and I could talk about science and watch documentaries with her. I'd never been with a woman like that before. I reckon that's what attracted me to her in the first place. I could see in Paula all the things I wished I could have been, and I wanted to be around that all the time. We were talking about getting married, maybe moving out of London to somewhere a bit more peaceful; maybe somewhere we could afford to buy a place of our own, and my life was starting to have a real plan to it for the first time. My mum fell in love with her before I did. She was waiting for some good woman to take over from her, is what I think. Paula was nothing like my mum, but I loved them both just the same.

I killed a person for a second time on a Monday morning at Tottenham Hale station. It was raining. This time the shock wasn't delayed. Someone had to help me do all the paperwork because my hands wouldn't stop shaking enough for me to use a pen. This one was an older man, in his forties, I would say. Again, I saw his face, but this time his eyes were closed and his hands were holding on to the top of his head, one hand sitting on top of the other. He must have been scared.

After everything was done and dusted, somebody was found to drive me home again and the boss told me not to come back for at least two weeks. I remember walking through the station to get to the car park. The platforms were full of people trying to get wherever they were going. All the trains, both directions, were delayed for more than an hour. I heard a couple of men in smart suits complaining that they'd be late for a meeting, swearing and cursing out loud at one of the station staff. I clenched my fists and carried on walking. I wanted to punch them.

They don't tell you the name of the person you've killed, even if you ask them for it. That way, it can't get personal. That way it's just another passenger on the line. You can't know why they wanted to die, what pushed them to do this terrible thing. But there are ways of finding out about people. Especially nowadays with social media and the internet. Everything's out there for anyone who cares to look. It didn't take me very long to find him.

His name was John Manderhill. He was fifty-four years old – older than he looked – and a husband with two children. Lucky for me, his surname was unusual so it was pretty easy to dig up information. His Facebook page settings were wide open. Definitely not a security conscious man. I sat in front of my computer for hours, scrolling down past all the messages of condolence to photographs of him on holiday with his wife and daughters; him at some work function in a shirt and tie but no jacket, arms around a couple of other guys, beer in their hands and red cheeks on their faces; a picture of a dog, it looked like a golden retriever, looking up at the camera with his tongue hanging out. I checked out everything he liked; his favourite bands were Status Quo and AC/DC and a third one I'd never heard of; his favourite film was *Goodfellas*; he shared bad jokes and pictures of hand-painted motorbikes. I found out where he went to school and the last company he worked for – some accountancy firm in the city. I scrolled and scrolled until I got to the end of his Facebook page; until I felt like I knew this man. He hadn't updated his page for a couple of months. The last status read: 'Happy birthday to the best wife in the world.'

I don't know what I was looking for. I guess I needed to know that he meant to be standing on those tracks in front of my train, that it was on purpose, but there was nothing. What did I expect? A public post saying: 'I'm going to kill myself today' or something? But there was nothing. No clue at all. Did he leave a note for his wife and children? I don't know. Why did he do it? All those posts and pictures online looked… well, normal, I guess. He could have been any guy down the pub.

Twice I sat down at the computer and wrote a private message for his wife on Facebook. The first one was long. I introduced myself and told her how sorry I was about her husband and how responsible I felt. I asked if there was any way that I could help or anything I could do. But I didn't send it. I read it three times and then I deleted it. The second time, the message was shorter. I just said I was sorry. My finger hovered over the keyboard while I read the words again and again, then I deleted that one too. I thought about searching for his address. It would be easy enough to find. I thought maybe I should send a card or some flowers, but I didn't.

John Manderhill became an obsession with me. I checked his Facebook page every day. His wife hadn't removed it. I found out that he had a Twitter account too, and I did the same with that. New messages appeared every day as friends of his heard the news and reached out to his family, sharing memories and pictures of better times when he was still with them. Then the funeral date was posted online. The service was going to be at a crematorium in Enfield. Paula didn't want me to go. She tried to understand. I know she did. She had long conversations with me about trauma and guilt and the need for closure, all those kinds of words that are easier to say than to do. It must have been really hard on her. I know she was right, but it didn't help. I knew all the theory, but that didn't stop the feelings. In the end, I didn't talk to her about it anymore because it always ended up in rows and frustration.

I wore my good black suit to the funeral. There was a ton of people there. Many more than there were when my dad was laid to rest. I sat at the back and watched. I recognised his wife and his children when they came in. His wife looked thinner than she did in the Facebook photos, and really, really tired. Not surprising, I guess. Several people spoke about what a great guy he was, lots of people cried into handkerchiefs, and then they played a song by Status Quo. I don't know what it was called. I'd never heard it before. I meant to go and talk to his wife, to introduce myself and say sorry to her face... but I couldn't. It was all too real. This wasn't on some flat, computer screen anymore. I sneaked out of the crematorium just as the coffin was sliding through the curtains and went home. I never looked at John Manderhill's Facebook page again.

When I got back home to the flat, Paula was gone. She left me a note to say that she just couldn't communicate with me anymore but I could call her anytime if I needed to talk. I called my boss instead and told him that I needed to take another two weeks off work. He thought it was a good idea.

When I turned up at my mum's house later that day, she didn't say anything. She just gave me a hug and put the kettle on. I sat in the kitchen and drank a cup of tea while mum did the washing up and cleaned the kitchen, although it was already spotless. Then I went up to my old room and stayed there for three days. Most of the time I just slept. The flashbacks and nightmares subsided a little bit more every day. They never completely leave you.

When I got back to work, I was pretty much ready to start again. They say that time is the best healer, and it's true, but you've got to be patient. The boss wouldn't let me drive for a couple of days, not until he was absolutely sure that I could handle it, but I had to get back on the train. If I didn't do it then, I would never be able to do it. He insisted that somebody else travel in the cab with me on the first journey, and I agreed. We talked about something and nothing all the way to the end of the line and, to be honest, I welcomed the distraction.

A day went by, and another and another, and time was indeed healing. Then one day, another driver from my depot hit a passenger on the line. My boss asked me to go round and talk to him, share my own experiences, and I did. I think it helped him, I don't know, but it definitely helped me. I was surprised about that. It made sense, though. It was the first time I'd really spoken out loud about what it's like to have someone step out in front of you like that, to use you as their weapon of choice. I spoke and things came out that I didn't know were there. They needed to come out. Some of it was tough, and some of it was useful, but it all helped. Maybe, if I'd found a way to do this in the first place, Paula would still be around.

Another day passed, then a week, then a year. The guilt and the trauma had shrunk down to a manageable size. There were good days and bad days, but I loved my job. I was proud to follow in the footsteps of my dad and his dad, and I always hoped that they'd be proud of me.

Then, yesterday, I was pulling in to Harlow Town station when another young man jumped in front of my train. It happened so fast. He was right at the end of the platform and he came out of nowhere. For the third time in my life I had killed another human being.

It doesn't get any easier. In fact, for me, it was even worse the third time. The shock hit me as hard as the train must have hit him, and I didn't stop shaking for the rest of the day. Part of me is still shaking inside. First was the horror, then came the anger, then the self-pity, and then… then I went numb. This time, the boss just put me into a car and said he would call me in a few days to talk about what I wanted to do next. As he closed the car door, he said: "Maybe it's time to think about a different career on the railways."

I went straight home, closed the curtains, and lay down on the sofa in the living room. I shut my eyes and tried to sleep, but it all kept flashing back through my mind. Every couple of minutes I saw the young man jumping in front of my train, then the other young man, then John Manderhill, over and over again, switching round and taking turns. I flicked on the TV so that I could focus on some other image. It was some shitty daytime show, but anything was better than what I saw when I closed my eyes. Sometime later, after it got dark outside, I finally fell asleep, still on the sofa with the TV on. I hadn't even taken off my shoes. Then the nightmares started. In the morning, it felt like I hadn't slept at all but every part of me was wide awake.

I hadn't eaten anything for twenty-four hours, but it didn't matter. I had a shower, got myself dressed, and left the flat. Something about being inside, within four walls, felt oppressive. It kind of felt safer to be outside where there was space. That doesn't make any sense but then, nothing did. I walked down the road, got on a bus and went to Liverpool Street station. I meant to go straight into the boss's office and talk to him about how I was feeling, but when I got to the station I panicked. He probably wasn't going to let me drive anymore, I knew that, and he would have been right, but I couldn't live with that thought. What would my father say? I felt like a failure.

So, I walked straight past the office towards the platforms and got on the first train that was waiting. I didn't even check to see where it was going. I didn't really care. A couple of stops later, I got off and got on another train. The further I travelled, the more the anxiety subsided and the more numb I became. It was like somebody had shot me full of anaesthetic. I got off that train and got on some other one, and another one, until eventually I got to Bury St Edmunds station.

It was cold, and it was getting dark and the station was pretty quiet. I walked right down to the end of the platform, as far as I could go without drawing attention to myself, and just stood there for a while so that I could be on my own and think.

I tried to imagine what it must have been like for all three men, for anyone who decides they want to jump in front of a moving train; to end their life like that, so violently. I don't know how long I stood there, but after a while the track started rattling and I could see the engine coming down the line. I took a step towards the edge of the platform, over the yellow safety lines, just to feel what it was like to be that close. I felt nothing. It wasn't that I wanted to jump, at least I don't think so, but I needed to understand what it takes for a man to do it. Maybe then it would all make sense and the guilt would go away. It wasn't my fault. I desperately needed to believe that. There was no way I could have stopped in time, not for any of them.

The track rattled louder and louder and the train got closer and closer, and I moved even nearer to the edge until I couldn't go any further without falling. The train was pulling in, almost on top of me… and then, the next thing I knew, some guy's rugby-tackling me to the ground and screaming in my face.

The train pulled in safely. No-one was hurt, just a bruise or two when I fell on my back. It woke me up, though. There was a driver in that train. Some man or woman just like me. Someone who was just doing their job. I didn't want to jump – honestly. I know that now. I would never have jumped. I just wanted everything to stop.

Chapter Twelve:
The Seventh Train to Peterborough

In the time it took Daniel Cotter to tell his story, three more trains had arrived and departed from Bury St Edmunds station. Nobody counted them out loud because it would have been rude to interrupt his flow. It was clear that he needed to talk and everyone in the waiting room, including Daniel, understood that. He'd started with a gush, apologising several times between sips of sweet tea, but once the initial shock died down he spoke slowly, making sure he was saying everything he wanted to. The others were patient and attentive and listened till he stopped.

Meanwhile, commuters from the town had finished work and filled both platforms before emptying themselves onto the trains. One or two passengers had pushed open the waiting room door during the storytelling, sensed the atmosphere inside, and left again hurriedly, closing the door behind them. Outside, the winter sky was dark, but the strip lights inside were bright and clinical and brought everything into sharp focus. The tension that had been apparent on Daniel's face had receded and his clenched hands were now relaxed and dropped down by his side. He looked exhausted.

Once she was sure he was finished, Ellie spoke first. "O-M-G. That's unbe-flippin-lievable," she said, dropping her weight against Elizabeth's shoulder as if she'd fallen sideways in amazement. Daniel just smiled weakly and nodded. "You know where you went wrong, don't you?" Ellie added. "You've been too random on the trains today. You should have got on the seventh one and then got off after four stops like us. It changes everything."

Daniel searched for clarity among the others. "What's she talking about?" he asked, bemused.

The next train to arrive at platform one is the seventeen-fifty-seven service to Cambridge, calling at Kennett, Newmarket and Cambridge. Platform one for the next service to Cambridge.

"Five!" cried Ellie, Barney, Ray and Elizabeth, all at once. They looked at each other with surprise then all burst out laughing. A moment of silliness was a welcome release after all the tragedy they'd been listening to.

"Allow me to explain," said Ray, sensing Daniel's unease at their outburst. Carefully and with his usual dramatic flair, he explained the rules of the seventh train with Barney interjecting here and there, just to make sure he was explaining it properly. Then Ray regaled them all with a summary of his own story, enjoying the recounting of it, like he always did, and adding little embellishments here and there. After Ray was satisfied, Barney volunteered a concise version of his story. He told it with a lot less drama but a little more heart than Ray, and Daniel seemed touched by what he heard.

Before anyone could ask for her story, Elizabeth excused herself, saying that she needed a coffee and was happy to get a hot drink for everyone else at the same time. She needed a little time to consider everything that was happening. The little café on platform one was just about to close, but the man behind the counter was affable and agreed to make one last round of drinks. He took himself into the small kitchen at the back and left Elizabeth to wait on her own in the empty café.

It would be very easy to slip away now and just walk out of the station before the seventh train arrived. There must be some nice little hotel in Bury St Edmunds that Elizabeth could check into for the night. Then she could come back in the morning and start counting again where she left off. The others wouldn't miss her for a while. By the time they did, she would have disappeared back into the town and become anonymous again. She had never intended to make this journey with anybody else. But then again, she had never expected to make a friend on her travels either. All she had really wanted was to be anywhere other than where she was. But, however many trains she boarded, and however many stations she arrived at, she couldn't escape from herself. Standing in a small café, in a Suffolk market town that she'd never been to before, she came to the realisation that it was alright to be where she was right at this moment. Maybe that was enough.

The equipment in the little café kitchen could only handle making one drink at a time. Elizabeth was glad that it was taking a while. She sat at the small table near the door and waited. She waited for the coffees, and she waited to find out what she was going to do next. It wasn't enough to think about it, she would have to trust her instincts. She reached into her handbag for her purse so that she was ready to pay when the coffees arrived. Her fingers found her little red diary instead. She'd almost forgotten that it was in there. The ribbon bookmark poked out from the bottom, marking a page near the beginning. She pulled at the ribbon, letting the diary fall open where it had been, and was suddenly confronted with the questions she had asked only four weeks ago. She stared at them, reading them back to herself, one word at a time:

'Q: Did you mean to kill yourself today? A: I don't know.'
'Q: Why didn't you jump? A: I don't know.'
'Q: Do you want to go back? A: No, there's nothing there.'
'Q: Where do you want to go? A: Nowhere.'

Back in the waiting room, Ellie and Barney were still trying to persuade Daniel to join them on the seventh train. "You can travel for free, can't you?" said Barney, "so it won't even cost you anything."

"Yes," confirmed Daniel, "or at least it's free with my company. I get a big discount on the other train lines, though."

"Can you get me discounts?" asked Barney. The small savings he had managed to accumulate in his working life were in danger of running out soon. He admitted to Daniel that he'd often managed to avoid paying by hiding in toilets or simply not leaving stations that had ticket barriers, preferring instead to sleep in waiting rooms overnight. "You won't report me, will you?"

"Don't worry," said Daniel. "I owe you one."

"You should have said if you were short, Barney," said Ray. "I can always help out. I'm loaded," he added, with neither embarrassment nor pretension. It was just a statement of fact. He was, indeed, loaded, thanks to *The Hot Cheese Sonata* and the royalties that continued to pour in from various merchandise deals.

"Thanks," said Barney. "That's good of you. I've got my Young Persons Railcard too."

"How long are you all going to travel like this?" asked Daniel.

"Until the money runs out," said Barney.

"Until the feeling runs out," replied Ray.

"Two weeks," said Ellie.

"Is that all?" said Daniel. "Then what?"

"Then I have to go back to work," explained Ellie. "Until then, I'm going to keep doing the seventh train. It's much better than just going to one place for my holidays. The world is my lobster!" She moved over on to the seat next to Daniel where Elizabeth had been sitting and put her hand on his knee. "Come on," she urged with a grin. "Come with us. Just till you feel better. You don't have to do it forever."

"Some of us might," said Barney.

"Some of us *will*," concluded Ray.

Daniel turned to take a good look at Ellie. When she smiled, she seemed to do it with her whole being. Her eyes were searching into his, crinkled at the sides from smiling. It was a warm smile. There was no danger in it. "I do need some time off," he conceded. "But I better give my mum a call. She'll worry if she doesn't hear from me." He reached into his pocket for his mobile phone. "I could tell her that I've gone away for a couple of weeks, maybe longer. She'll understand."

"Yay!" cried Ellie, slapping Daniel on the knee and moving back on to the arm of the couch. "He's coming with us, Barney."

Ray slapped Daniel on the back, as if to say, 'welcome aboard, son.' Barney got up from his seat and held out his hand. Daniel stood up for the first time since he'd been helped into the waiting room by the two men. He took Barney's hand and shook it warmly. "Thank you, brother" he said. "I was never going to jump in front of that train, I couldn't have done that to another driver. But I think you saved my life all the same. I'll never forget it."

The waiting room door opened and Elizabeth entered with a cardboard tray full of coffees. She passed them round and took her seat back on the couch. "I was getting worried about you," said Ellie, cradling the hot coffee cup gratefully in her cold hands. "I thought you might have done a runner." She took a loud slurp of her coffee, let out a high-pitched Eek!' and fanned at her mouth with her hand. It was hot.

The next train to arrive at platform two is the eighteen-twenty-six service to Ipswich, calling at Thurston, Elmswell, Stowmarket, Needham Market and Ipswich. Platform two for the next service to Ipswich.

There was a pregnant pause in the waiting room as the announcement rang out over the tannoy. "Six!" said Ellie.

"Six!" cried Barney and Ray together.

All eyes turned towards Daniel. He put his hand on Barney's shoulder. "Six," he said. Smiles and cheers were shared all round as the men shook hands and slapped backs again while Ellie clapped encouragement.

Nobody noticed that Elizabeth had said nothing. She sat back and surveyed the scene as the others chatted, comparing notes and sipping coffees. Daniel broke off into the corner briefly to call his mother and reassure her that he was OK; just taking some time off to repair. Ellie fished her travel journal out of her bag and showed it to Barney. She borrowed a pen from Ray and wrote her first entry, him making suggestions as to how she might improve her writing style as she went along. Then Daniel came back and Ray turned to him instead, for which Ellie was grateful. She wanted to record things in her own way. "Did you ever see *The Hot Cheese Sonata?*" Ray asked his new friend.

Elizabeth watched them all. It was such an odd assortment of human beings that she had somehow, by some quirk of fate, found herself in the company of: an eccentric movie maker, a gardener with a conscience, a traumatised train driver, and Ellie... Ellie, for whom the world was her lobster. Ellie full of awe and wonder, full of the spirit of adventure, gaily striding into the unknown without fear or judgement. She was the girl that Elizabeth never was; the girl that Elizabeth now understood she'd always wished to be. She took out the red diary and pen and opened the page that was still marked with the ribbon. Elizabeth crossed out the answer to the last question, and wrote 'Everywhere!' instead. Quietly, and without anyone else noticing, she whispered, "Six," and put the diary back into her bag.

Outside the waiting room on the opposite platform, a random array of passengers were boarding the train to Ipswich. The seventh train was due not far behind.

The next train to arrive at platform one is the eighteen-twenty-nine service to Peterborough, calling at Ely, March, Whittlesea and Peterborough. Platform one for the next service to Peterborough.

"Seven!" cried Ellie. "Come on," she urged the others, shoving her travel journal back into her bag.

"Seven!" cried Barney, Ray and Elizabeth.

"Do we really have to call out like this every time?" asked Daniel.

"Yes!" answered Ellie. "It makes it more fun."

All personal belongings were gathered together and the growing band of travellers left the warmth of the waiting room and stepped out onto platform one. The icy wind bit into bare skin, and Elizabeth pulled her jacket a bit tighter around herself. Ellie felt the cold too and slid her hand under the crook of Elizabeth's arm, tucking herself close in beside her.

Barney took the big suitcase from Ellie so that she could huddle even closer to Elizabeth. She thanked him for noticing that she was cold and promised that she'd pack a much smaller suitcase if she ever did this again. "No problem," said Barney. "That's a point." Barney turned to Ray. "How come you don't have any luggage?"

"Oh, I do," he said dismissively. "I just got fed up with carrying it around. I've got small overnight bags stored in railway lockers up and down the country. I just pick them up when I need them. I hope I end up in Birmingham again soon. I could do with my thermal long johns," he added wistfully.

Ellie wasn't sure if he was joking or not. She decided to take him at his word. "Do you think there are other people getting together on the trains like us?" she asked the group.

"Who knows?" shrugged Ray.

"I've never come across it before," said Daniel, "and I've worked on the trains for years. You never know," he added, "maybe lots of people are doing it and I just never noticed."

"I like the thought of that," cooed Ellie. "Lots of people all over the world, getting on the seventh train, making friends with strangers. It's kind of odd though, ain't it?"

"Very," agreed Elizabeth.

"And we'll all ride off into the sunset," said Ray, sweeping the air with his hand, "and live happily ever after with season tickets."

"Group tickets are cheaper," said Daniel. "I'll see if I can sort something out for you all."

The track began its low rattle, getting louder and louder as the train to Peterborough approached Bury St Edmunds. A random assortment of other passengers dotted the platform in little clumps, readying themselves to get on the train, all keen to get out of the cold and into an empty seat. Maybe one or two of them had counted 'seven' before getting on, blissfully unaware that they weren't the only ones.

The train eased into the station and everyone began to move towards whichever door happened to be closest. They opened in unison with a 'swoosh.' All passengers boarded, all doors closed, a whistle blew and the train moved on. The woman with the perfect voice addressed the station through the tannoy, like she did at all the stations, whether there was anyone there or not:

This is a passenger safety announcement. Please ensure that all luggage and personal items are kept with you at all times and report any suspicious activity to staff at the station security office. Thank you for travelling with us today.

Fortunately, the carriage wasn't too full. As the Seventh Trainers settled themselves down, spreading out across two empty tables, Ellie squeezed Elizabeth's arm. "This is just the beginning," she said.

"No," corrected Ray. "This is just the middle."

Epilogue:
Union Station, Los Angeles

The sun was shining fiercely over Union Station. It was almost always shining in California, to the point where it was becoming tedious. If it weren't for the occasional clouds of smog, the colour of the Los Angeles sky would have hardly any variation at all. Virtually no-one ever discussed the weather in California. There was really not much point.

For some, celebrity spotting is a sport in LA, not least at Union Station. There are many virtual points to be scored by snapping a candid shot of some Hollywood luminary or Reality TV star in the corner of a selfie, that's then shamelessly posted on social media for others to celebrate or mock in equal measure. Ms Mabel Heep – like so many other movie stars at her elite, A-list level – was familiar with all the tricks used by these celebrity trophy hunters. She'd seen it, done it, and made the acceptance speech many, many times.

Once, Ms Heep had been approached by a young, up-and-coming starlet, thrust into the limelight too quickly and forced to justify poorly-judged teenage tweets and sleazy, low-budget films done 'just for the money' during her early career. The starlet in question – who shall remain nameless for legal reasons – asked the seasoned Ms Heep for tips on handling the media. "The best advice I can give you, honey, is this," said La Heep. "Never allow yourself to be photographed with a drink in your hand."

It was mid-afternoon under that relentless, California sun, and Mabel Heep had just got out of a taxi carrying a small, neat overnight bag in one hand and a large, faux-lizard designer bag in the other. Her much-admired mane of blonde hair was neatly tucked under a curly auburn wig, which in turn was crowned by a wide-brimmed, soft cream sun hat. A subtly expensive pair of sunglasses covered her pale blue eyes and her equally pale face looked far more youthful than its years, considering Ms Heep was wearing no make-up at all except for the merest hint of lip gloss. Her light grey, linen trouser suit was smartly tailored and her shoes were flat, comfortable and overpriced. She was a picture of achingly ordinary, healthy, California middle-aged affluence. No-one would have looked at her twice. That's just how she liked it – when she wasn't doing the job that she was exceedingly well paid for.

Union Station was always busy, even in the middle of the week in the middle of the afternoon. Mabel Heep stepped through the main doors into the cavernous entrance lobby. It was a vision of Art Deco elegance with its shiny mosaic floor, dripping chandeliers and comfy, brown leather armchairs. The clatter of voices and trolley wheels and heels on hard flooring echoed around the hall and up into its splendid high ceiling. Every inch of the place was clean and shiny, mopped and swept almost continuously, it seemed, by a small army of uniformed service staff. Ms Heep walked straight on through, past tourists and commuters and shoeshine men, enjoying the coolness of the air conditioning after the heat from outside.

She was in no rush today; no rehearsal to get to, no script to read, no scene to shoot, so Mabel Heep decided to stop at 'Coffee Universe' and grab a coffee on her way through the station. She was the third person in the queue, so there was just time to have a think about which accent she would use for her coffee order today – Ms Heep was renowned for her genius with an accent. From Southern Belle to Russian Bond girl, she could do them all and juggle props at the same time. Her disguise today was obviously perfect, no-one had batted an eyelid at her, but that would be pointless if they could recognise her voice. 'Perhaps an English accent might be fun today,' she thought to herself.

The young, perfectly-groomed, young man behind the coffee counter flashed a flawless smile at Ms Heep. He moved and spoke like he was being secretly filmed for a commercial. Clearly another resting actor just trying to pay the rent until a big part came along. The coffee shops in LA were almost exclusively staffed by them. "Good day, ma'am. What can I get ya?" he drawled.

"May I please have a black coffee, decaff. Regular size, thank you," she purred in her best *Downton Abbey* voice.

The barista raised his eyebrows and enquired, a little over-enthusiastically: "Oh, are you from Australia, ma'am?"

Mabel Heep bristled. "No, young man. I'm British, actually." Couldn't he tell? Her English accent was one she was particularly proud of. It had garnered rave reviews when she used it in her bodice-ripping blockbuster, *Viva Queen Victoria*. This boy obviously had no class.

"I'm sorry. Decaff, did you say?"

"Yes – please," and Ms Heep emphasised the last word in a last-ditch attempt to sound as English as possible.

They always say 'Please' and 'Thank you' too easily. It had taken all her self-control not to say 'Don't you know who I am?' but she was glad she'd held back. She reasoned to herself that she'd had far worse reviews than this, took her coffee and made her way through the station towards the ticket office of the sprawling building.

American railway announcements are quite different to British ones. For one thing, they're much friendlier in tone. Polite with just the right amount of formality, perhaps, but never too snobbish and certainly not condescending. The Americans hate that, unless it comes from one of their British cousins, and then they find it terribly endearing. Despite the affable politeness, the train announcers hardly ever say 'please' or 'thank you' either. It's deemed unnecessary when making a statement of fact. An attitude that the British find bewildering.

"Good afternoon. May I have your attention. Passengers travelling Southbound on Surfliner 782: this train is now boarding on track nineteen. This train will make station stops at Fullerton, Anaheim, Santa Ana, Irvine, San Juan Capistrano, Oceanside, Solano Beach, Old Town and Downtown San Diego. Once again: We are now boarding Southbound Surfliner 782 on track nineteen. This train will depart at four-o-eight pm. All aboard."

Mabel Heep lowered her sunglasses, resting them on the end of her surgically-perfect nose so that she could take a quick peek at the digital departure boards. She made a quick scan of the various destinations, stretching out all across the country, then slid her sunglasses back into place and took a sip of coffee. Hoisting her designer bag up onto her shoulder, Mabel Heep strolled casually towards the waiting platforms. "One," she said.

Appendix

During the year 2017/18, there were 292 suicides or suspected suicides on the UK rail network. 249 on mainline rail and 43 on the underground. This is an increase of 9.1% on the previous year.

(Office of Rail and Road statistics)

The Samaritans are available at the end of a phone, 24 hours a day, 365 days a year. Calls are free, and you don't have to be suicidal to call. If you know somebody that might need to talk, the number in the UK or Republic of Ireland is 116 123.

And if you want to support *The Samaritans* in the essential charity work that they do, there is information on ways you can help at www.samaritans.org